Show Them What They Won

Sean Boling

Published by Sean Boling, 2017.

SHOW THEM WHAT THEY WON

First edition. January 3, 2017.

Copyright © 2017 Sean Boling.

ISBN: 979-8224381203

Written by Sean Boling.

CHAPTER 1

"I feel really bad for what happened to those kids, but..."

"It's sad what happened to those kids, but..."

"What happened to those kids was awful, but..."

But.

But.

But.

The children, those beautiful children, had been turned into an introductory phrase. They were preludes to a counter-argument. Nameless. Faceless. Instead of Cameron, Abby, Luis, Mona, Nate, and Stanley, his beautiful Stanley, they were "With All Due Respect" and "Don't Get Me Wrong".

He wished they wouldn't bother with the preamble. Anyone who said they felt bad didn't really feel bad, or awful, or sad. They couldn't. No one truly can.

Unless it happens to their child. Unless theirs is one of the little bodies being waved away as a lead-in to a claim that there's nothing we can do to stop it from happening again.

"Just cut to the point," he would think. "And be honest. Say what's really in your heart. 'Sorry, kids, but I love guns. God damn, do I love guns. They're who I am. I don't know what I'd do without them.'"

"Just admit it," he would think.

Because unless you've read or heard that your neighborhood school is breaking news, waited for the best part of your life to emerge from the crowd, waited for your favorite person in the world to run toward you and hug you...

Unless you've had to identify the body that generated all the light and energy in your life, cleaned and put back together for presentation, more beautiful than ever...

Unless you've tried to memorize that beauty before the sheet is drawn, wondering if that's really a memory you want, but hungry for any memory you can get...

"Unless you've been through that," he would think, "I would prefer you shut up. You are taking their names in vain."

"The Children" was a recitation, a memorized prayer blurted out before eating, or going to bed.

It wasn't much better on the other side, when the gun haters used the kids. They were groveling. They tried too hard to care, when they could never understand any more than their opponent.

For a while, Stanley's school was the latest "We Are". We Are Orlando. We Are Newtown. We Are This Place. We Are That Place. We Are Posting This On Our Facebook Page. We Are Grocery Shopping. We Are Driving To Work. We Are Choosing a Pair of Shoes. We Are Forgetting What We Are. He reminded himself of their good intentions every time he saw one of those slogans. But they also reminded him of what happened. And they were everywhere. It was such an easy thing for people to do. It was too easy. When he was having an especially bad day, when a reason to live was hard to come by and anger and sadness were all he had to rely on to help him find one, he saw those posts as an attempt to show off. All people wanted was to show what great people they were. And he would hate himself for thinking that. He didn't want to give up on humankind. Plenty had been so compassionate, had grieved with him as best they could.

And when their best fell short, the botched attempt helped in its own odd way. A world where too many people felt the way he did was no world worth living in. It was a relief to know there was a larger group of relatively happy people who could keep the machines and institutions running. On better days he was grateful for the shallow show of solidarity.

New events were executed. More "We Are" slogans accumulated. Others were forced to understand how he felt.

The children continued to be an abstraction to all concerned. People would mention the kids, then move on to what they saw as the larger point they were trying to make. To him, there was nothing larger than what happened to Stanley and his classmates. When he thought of Stan, he was done for a while. He was pinned. He would try so hard to forget what happened that day, to fight the visions of what it must have been like inside that room. He would try so hard to keep his mind away from that day, his brain ceased all other functions.

"Someone should design a bumper sticker or a web thingy that just says, 'We Are,'" he said. "Don't even put a place after it. I think we're reaching a point where people would get it."

"You're probably right," I agreed. "Sadly."

I was surprised to find out the shooting was the reason he contacted me. I had told that story already, and didn't want to tell it again.

"He had an old man's name," he said as he rose from the table in his hotel room. "It was so fitting. He was an old soul, as they say."

He paced and turned away from me to remove his sunglasses and rub his eyes. He put them back on and reached under his hoodie to scratch his head, then worked on his beard.

"Did they frisk you at the front desk?" he sat back down.

I shook my head.

"Good for them," he said. "Pushing back against the paranoia."

There was no need to be searched. The parking lot was almost empty, save for the cars driven by employees. The courtyard in the center of the hotel was primed for guests who were not coming. The pool, outdoor fireplaces, deck chairs were immaculate but unused. There was no one to shoot.

"It's bad enough the rooms are so cheap nowadays," he continued. "You want a water?"

"No, thank you."

"Rooms used to go for triple what they're getting. Ag tourism, wine trails, bed and breakfasts. Or would it be beds and breakfast? Which one is plural?"

"I'd go with the second word in this case. Bed and breakfasts."

"Now we're lumped in with all the 'rural violence'. Now we're just 'the country', and all that implies these days. But why am I telling you this? You've been around here long enough to remember."

I nodded.

"Sorry," he continued. "My relationship with time is frayed. Things can change so quickly. In a matter of seconds. And in a matter of years we've gone back to the Middle Ages, it seems. As though the cities have walls around them and the countryside is filled with dark forests and highwaymen."

"Why am I here?"

He seemed to have to remind himself why he had invited me to this room.

"I like your work," he finally said. "You still have hope."

"I write about hopeful things. Those are my assignments. The shooting was an exception, and only because it was local."

"You're not as hopeful as your work?"

"I don't know."

"Your work brought you to me."

"Whatever that means."

He chuckled.

"Awfully arrogant of me. I seem to think that because I've suffered, I've become wise."

He stroked his beard again.

"Not sure why I'm bothering with this," he said about his beard, then pulled off his hood. "I'm not going to hide anything from you. Habit, I guess. Or maybe I've given up. It's more about grooming than lying low. Lying or laying?"

"Remember earlier? When I asked why I was here?"

"I do," he smiled. "I've been sitting on this story for too long. I'm anxious to tell it, but scared."

"I'm a small town reporter."

"You won't be after I'm done with you. Or you're done with me. I'm done with myself."

He fell silent. It was hard to tell if he was looking back at me. He still had his sunglasses on. He tilted his head and appeared to be mildly surprised that I was there.

"Do you remember those theories about a possible 'shooter zero', the one who started it all?" he asked.

"Vaguely," I answered. "Not really my beat. I was busy interviewing 4-H scholarship winners."

He shook his head and waved in my direction, assuring me I hadn't shirked my duties as a reporter by not being familiar with it.

"The story never grew legs," he said.

Then he sunk into a grave stillness.

"It should have."

He let his statement hang there for a while, suspended between us.

I was done coaxing. He had called me, praised my work, claimed he had a career-altering story to tell. He needed to show me something. I waited, somewhat patiently.

"I'm a monster," he said. "One of those rumors. Bigfoot, The Abominable Snowman. Ah. I like that one. It uses the word 'abominable.'"

I slid my phone out from my back pocket.

"May I record you?" I asked. "Or would you prefer I just take notes?"

"Do it all," he said. "Make me real."

I tapped on the red button. I opened my notebook, uncapped my pen, and suspended it above the blank page.

He took off his sunglasses.

CHAPTER 2

Hart preferred to walk alone, but he didn't mind running into Nando. They were both retired police officers. The town was full of retired cops. It was beautiful country and within the budget of a well-negotiated pension. Their favorite walk was the one where they exited the housing tract they lived in through an archway in the wall on one side of the development, walked along the city limit, and reentered through an opening on the other side. The sidewalk skirting the city grid functioned as sort of a track on which they would take their lap.

The boundary was quite pronounced. On one side of the street was the sidewalk lined with rosemary bushes and boxwood, crabapple trees rising from the hedgerow every ten yards, and the two-story and one-story homes alternating behind the wall that ran alongside the landscaping. The wall had evidence of ivy. The tendrils remained stuck to it, but the leaves would burn off in the summer and freeze off in the winter, so usually the only thing clinging to the plaster were the shadowy veins. The other side of the street had no sidewalk. It was open meadow, with some hills erupting from it on the near horizon. Vineyards ran up some of the slopes, while cows grazed on the others. An occasional driveway marked with a mailbox would run through a ranch to a house that was usually hidden in a grove of trees. Some homes were visible. None were next to the street.

Hart had put in his twenty five years and was done before age fifty. Retirement at a relatively young age introduced him to how easy it was to feel aimless. He was concerned with being a burden, even though he was a long way from being one. He felt older than he was. Spending two and a half decades interacting with the most infuriating members of society had also aged him. It dimmed his view of the world, starting with the city he had worked in. People from out of town would ask him where they could grab a bite to eat in a certain district, and he'd tell them not to bother, it was full of abusers and thieves. They would ask about another area, and he would say the same thing but with different words. Even the trendy neighborhoods. He knew what went on in the back of those businesses. He knew who overextended themselves and took it out on their families. Human sharks swam at every depth, as far as he was concerned.

His marriage was in trouble even before the shooting. His wife thought getting away from his job and from the city would help. And it did for a while. But that was more thanks to their grandson than the town they retired in.

Stanley is what made life better.

Their daughter and her husband moved nearby after Stanley was born. The husband was able to keep his lucrative job in the tech industry by telecommuting. The beautiful young family lived in one of those hidden ranch homes.

"We have achieved perfection," Hart would say to his wife after a day with Stanley.

"You're being rewarded for the time you put in," she would say to him.

Then Stanley was murdered, with sixteen of his classmates, and the swamp rose again.

So Hart walked religiously. When he held still, he heard all the filthy voices he thought he had put behind him saying "Welcome back."

He had no photographs of Stanley. His wife had taken all the pictures with her phone when they were together, and took them all with her when she left.

He did have one video saved in his camera. It was only six seconds. Stanley had taken it himself on the Sunday before his last day. Four seconds were of Hart, and only two were of his grandson. Stanley was in all six seconds if you counted his foot.

They are both seated at the kitchen table. Stanley had spent the night at grandma and grandpa's house. He points the camera at Hart, who sits across from him. Hart is reading the Sunday paper, the only old-fashioned version of a newspaper he still subscribed to. Since he didn't need to use his phone to catch up on the news that morning, he let Stanley play with it. Stan's foot peaks out from the bottom of the frame.

"Grandpa," he says. "My foot is on the table again."

Hart pretends to be annoyed with a sigh, without looking up from his reading.

Stanley fake laughs, and turns the camera on himself.

The six seconds expire with a blurry freeze frame of Stanley in mid-laugh.

Some days he would see if he could make it through a day without watching those six seconds. Other days he would see how many times he could watch it.

His record was three hundred and twelve.

He paused long enough one day to meet Nando, who understood the job, and thanks to that could almost understand the shooting, could come closer than most who had no love taken from them.

But Hart kept walking away from his wife. She rekindled a friendship with a man in their old town and moved back when it turned into something more. She left in a hurry, took nothing but her belongings, and left him the house. It was too much house for one person, but it was full of natural light, and didn't wear its history. It was still so new and so similar to the homes around it. Hart looked into downsizing, but the condos and apartments he visited felt like surrender. He was grateful to his wife, happy for her, and relieved.

He found an upside to how forlorn the house could be, since that offered further inspiration to get out and walk. If he could stay healthy, he could put off being a nuisance to his daughter. She and her husband were still together. Their marriage survived the massacre. Though he wasn't sure how much time they actually spent in each other's company.

"Megan travels a lot for her job," Hart answered when Nando asked how things were going with his daughter.

"She gets paid to do what she does?"

Hart knew Nando wasn't a fan of Megan's mission. Nando had an impressive gun collection that he seemed to love more than his wife, maybe even more than his kids, who had grown up in disappointing fashion. When it came to Nando's love, it was probably a tie between his guns and his dog.

"Yeah," Hart said. "They used her as a prop at first. 'Bring on the weeping mother.' But they saw she's got a talent for getting things done."

He decided to take a dig at Nando.

"And she's getting things done alright," he dug. "They tightened up the concealed carry requirements in some county, I think in Montana. And they're pretty sure they've got a buyback program ready to roll in New Mexico somewhere."

"Well," Nando took a few strides to choose his response. "Good for her."

Hart almost laughed. He managed to channel it into some puffs of exertion instead.

He wasn't sure whose side he was on at that point. During his career, he had no doubts. He saw enough danger on all fronts to hold fast to the right to bear arms. He saw danger in the charred souls they pursued, and in some of his colleagues who abused their power in that pursuit. He sympathized both with those who feared the more immediate threats of intruders, of mug shots on the news, and with those who feared the more abstract threats of tyranny, of a government they fancied as something out of a dystopian science fiction trilogy.

But his grandson's murder grabbed him and shook him up, rattling the beliefs around inside of him.

He cheered on his daughter's quest in spite of his indifference to the issue as it hovered over the culture. The matter had been turned into a spectator sport. Its fans really had nothing to lose. Few were affected personally by what they rooted for or against. Some were. But they were at a distance. The victims and their families were players on a field, out there, under the lights.

Sports fans struck him as ultimately more rational. They knew a lot about their opponents, and studied them to find ways to make their team better. Gun debate teams made up stories about their opponents. He continued to monitor their posturing for Megan's sake. It gave her purpose, and might have made her feel better, if that was possible.

"Who's that?" Nando nodded ahead of them toward Hart's house.

Megan's husband was parked in the driveway, leaning against his car.

"My son-in-law, Quentin."

Quentin stood upright and fidgeted as they approached.

"You can invite me in next time," Nando said as they drew closer to Hart's house and Quentin grew more uncomfortable.

Hart veered off the sidewalk onto the path that led to his door and gave Nando a wink, who waved back, and then waved at Quentin. Hart turned to see Quentin briefly raise a hand in response before burying both his hands in his pockets.

"What's up, Q? Run out of coffee?"

"No, no," Quentin hedged. "Got plenty. Just hoping you could talk."

"I've got nothing but time," Hart gestured for him to follow.

They went inside and reached the kitchen. The pot of coffee Hart had started before he left on his walk was ready.

"I know you've got your own," Hart said as he poured some into a mug that commemorated the Toys for Tots program his department helped sponsor. "But can I interest you in some of mine?"

"I'm good. I'm good."

"Have a seat."

Quentin sat at the kitchen table but seemed ready to spring back up. He didn't like people much, but resented the anti-social stereotypes projected onto the tech industry, and worked hard at being friendly. Sometimes too hard.

"You seem like you've had several cups already," Hart said as he sat down across from him. "Something I can help you with?"

"Oh, boy," Quentin exhaled. "Oh boy, can you. You sure can."

Hart waited for him to continue. He took a sip of coffee to give Quentin some more time.

"Well?" he finally asked.

"Well..." Quentin took another deep breath and tapped the table. "Well, well, well."

"Everything okay with Megan?"

"No. I mean, yes. Between us, fine. We're fine."

"That's good. She wouldn't tell me if there was a problem. She still relies on her mother for those kinds of conversations."

"It's her job."

"I suppose," Hart took a sip. "I think even sons prefer to talk to their mothers about relationship stuff."

"I mean Megan's job."

"What about it?"

"That's the problem. When you asked me if everything was okay with Megan, and I said no, that's what I was talking about."

"I was under the impression it's going well."

"She certainly thinks so," Quentin started to settle down as he reached the purpose of his visit.

"You don't see it that way?"

"Drops in the bucket. Grains of sand on the beach. Pick your metaphor."

"I thought that was the strategy. Go local. Build from the ground up."

"It is," Quentin sighed. "It is."

"And you think that's a bad idea."

"They kid themselves. They can line up all these accomplishments, all the laws they've helped pass. Great raw numbers, but when you zoom out and look at their market share..."

He spat out a fart noise and gave a thumbs-down sign.

"Always the data analyst," Hart raised his mug and toasted him.

"Sorry," Quentin leaned back as if to reset his pitch. "Staying as rational as possible about our situation is how I fill the hole."

"Just teasing, Q. That's how I get by."

They respected each other in silence, a long sip's worth, enough for a couple of birds outside the window to come to a verbal agreement of some sort.

"I'm proud of Megan," Hart said. "It's a tough business she's in."

"You're right," Quentin was re-energized by the situation being referenced in business terms. "Advocacy is tough enough. Make it about guns, it's next to impossible."

"All the more reason to be proud of what she's accomplished," Hart tried to keep the conversation positive.

Quentin wouldn't bite.

"What makes it so hard?" he rhetorically asked Hart.

"Just tell me your answer," Hart sighed. "You clearly have one in mind."

"People can't talk about it. Not rationally."

"True."

"We get nowhere fast. We've got about ten seconds before we start shouting at each other, or start typing in all capital letters with a dozen exclamation marks after every sentence."

"Before it gets emotional."

"It's emotional all the time," Quentin was leaning on the table more than he was sitting in the chair. "We come up with reasons after we've already made up our minds. People either see guns as the only thing standing between them and chaos, or as the agents of chaos. Some can sound rational for a while as they regurgitate their prepared statements. But that's just a facade. Wisdom has nothing to do with it."

"Are you saying one side is more reasonable?" Hart felt his old guard going up.

"No," Quentin leaned back. "I'm saying you can't change people's minds who are emotionally attached to a position."

"Can't ever?"

"Not with reason, not with logic. Only if you change their emotions. Look at you."

"Okay..."

"Or more to the point, look at Stanley."

Hart glared at him.

"We get it," Quentin explained. "Both of us. Our emotional connection to the issue is undeniable. If we had stopped a home invasion by firing a gun, our feelings would be on the other side. But our boy was killed by one, so here we stand. We can't hide from our emotions. Other people pretend they're logical. We know better."

"Megan and her team use plenty of emotion in their presentations."

"Pointless."

"You just said..."

"Their emotional appeals are at a distance. They're abstract. They only work on those who already agree with them. Those on the other side see right through them. If you're with them, you get a tear in your eye and your biases confirmed. If you're against them, you call bullshit."

"How does this involve me? Is there something you want me to tell Megan?"

"No," Quentin snapped. "Quite the contrary. This stays between us."

"Well," Hart held up his hands in surrender. "Okay then. What is this? This thing that's not supposed to leave the room?"

Quentin suddenly looked as though he hadn't slept in weeks, as though he had been doing his best impression of a conscious person, and had finally broken character.

"More people who love guns need to hate them. Hate them as much as we do. A visceral, instinctual hatred that sticks to them, that haunts their days and their dreams."

"You want me to kill their kids?" Hart tried to shock him back into the waking world.

But Quentin took it in stride.

"Not you," he said. "No. You don't have to kill anyone."

Hart released his grip on his mug, put both hands on the table, and leaned back.

"You?" he annunciated slowly. "You're going to kill kids?"

"Not kids," Quentin woke up. "God, no. But...people. Yes."

Hart bowed his head.

"People who love guns," Quentin clarified.

"And then other people who love guns won't love them anymore?" Hart kept his head down.

"They'll have been hurt by them."

"What if their guns send them flowers?"

"Dammit, Hart..."

"Then again, in an abusive relationship, that's usually not even necessary."

"I'm serious..."

"We'd respond to these domestic abuse calls, and as we're taking the husband away, the wife would come out and start hitting us."

"I need you to train me, Hart."

Hart looked up.

"I would never implicate you," Quentin pleaded. "If someone found out we were at the shooting range together, I'd say I asked you to train me for home security."

"That's a load off my mind."

Hart shivered and stood up, walking off what he heard.

"I've thought this through," Quentin stood up and came around the table to face Hart. "I need your help."

"I can't give you the kind of help you need," Hart braced himself at the counter. "I thought you were seeing a therapist."

"I am."

"You need a new one."

"I'm not crazy. What's crazy is letting things go on the way they are and fooling ourselves into thinking we're making a difference."

Hart was through answering back for the moment. He worked on settling himself down while Quentin ranted on, pacing the kitchen floor.

"Like these buyback programs Megan gets all excited about. Even if thousands of people show up and pitch their guns onto the pile, how many more do they have at home? How many of those guns are even theirs? How many of them really care? They just want a few bucks. Times are tough. And those laws she helps get passed. The gun lovers are right. They don't mean a thing. Not a damn thing. Even if Megan and her non-profit and every other competing Moms Who Hate Guns organization got their way in every statehouse and every courtroom across the country, we've still got more guns than people. We're saturated in them. We're soaked. And they're not going anywhere. We can't make them disappear. Nobody's signature can make that happen. People still need to take them away or get rid of them. And how many people want to do that? A disgusting number of people enjoy the slaughter. They don't say so out loud, but they do. They see it as evidence. Numbers. They're rooting for the end of civilization because it means they can finally use their guns. They dream of a chance to roam the streets armed with everything in their basement stockpile."

Hart grabbed Quentin by the shoulders and stared him down.

"You're right," he said as steadily as he could manage. "And you're undermining your own argument. There is no amount of violence that will convince some people. More carnage? We need more guns. Less carnage? Guns are working. You're cornered, Q. Their answer is always the same, always will be."

"That's because they haven't felt the blood that's been spilled," Quentin maintained. "If we change their world, we change their worldview."

Hart loosened his grip.

"Let Megan do what she does," he said. "Celebrate the small victories. But the war is over. They won. They may not realize it. Not by the way they talk. But you know it. That's why you've come up with this insane idea. You feel helpless. I understand."

He patted one of Quentin's shoulders before letting them both go.

Quentin didn't seem to notice.

"Then let's show them what they won," he said.

Hart sighed.

Quentin continued.

"If they see the real cost of the world they want, and still don't feel ashamed, so be it. I'll concede. But they need to know the feeling."

"Go home, Q."

"To what?"

"Oh, please. Look who you're talking to."

"Our house is as empty as yours."

"Your wife is coming home."

"In a manner of speaking," Quentin scoffed.

Hart crossed his arms and fell back against the counter, as though conducting a trust exercise.

"Have you asked Megan to stop?" he asked. "Or slow down, at least?"

Quentin rolled his eyes.

Hart hung his head and let it nod.

They stood quietly and avoided eye contact, like a couple who had just broken up.

When Quentin spoke, he sounded like he had finished addressing a stadium full of people, with little voice left to hold a conversation.

"Our lives are hopelessly linked to this goddamn issue," he said. "I want to go all in. Settle it once and for all."

"I can't help you, Q."

Quentin shrugged.

"Thanks for listening," he said, and headed for the entryway.

"If I get wind of you pursuing this," Hart called after him. "I'll stop you."

Quentin paused at the front door.

"You were my only chance," he said as he opened it.

He walked out and closed the door behind him.

Hart stayed in the same position for some time, wondering if he should call his daughter.

CHAPTER 3

He resisted telling Megan what her husband had told him.

Hart had a feeling that what Quentin really wanted to do was kill himself. If he followed through on his plan, it would be suicide. The first time Quentin confronted some doomsday prepper or tried to stalk a militia member, it would be over. Hart could teach him to handle a weapon, but he wouldn't be able to handle himself. He would freeze from fear, or miss from anger. And even if he chose a victim who was just as jumpy as he was, being attacked would press that person into action.

If Quentin was in fact suicidal, Hart wouldn't be the only one to notice. Megan would pick up on it. The signals would be different, he wouldn't run the same bit of lunacy by her, but he would reveal himself in other ways. So Hart decided to maintain Quentin's trust. By doing so, he could keep him close, keep track of him, while Megan made her own discoveries.

He increased his walking. Not long after his morning lap along the city limits with Nando, he was off again, heading in the opposite direction toward the business district. He would pass a vacant lot across a busy street from the box stores that kept their distance from the downtown restaurants and boutiques, as if each type of business had their turf, where they mingled with their own kind. Staked on the vacant lot was a sign proclaiming the pending construction of a senior living facility.

An article in the local news concerning the facility caught his attention. The development company was to have their building permit hearing before the city council.

Hart was curious. He wanted to see what he would be walking past in the near future, and where he might be living in a slightly more distant future.

Attending the city council meeting made him feel like quite the retiree. He thought this was the sort of thing people do who are looking to fill their days and who feel their role in the world diminishing. And for a presentation regarding an assisted living residence, no less.

His encounter with Quentin had convinced him to act more like his retired brethren. Hart felt helpless after their conversation, unable to help him or his daughter, unable to make a difference. It was time to appreciate the time he had left. Feeling distressed about the condition of the world is a logical part of growing older, he told himself. Sure, we may say we want to leave the world better than we found it, but actually believing the world is getting better is depressing. We won't be around to take part in it. So we tell ourselves it was better back whenever, and we won't be missing much when we die.

Hart watched a line of people older than him prove his point. One by one they proclaimed their anger. They felt the town was getting too big, even though most of them had contributed to that by moving there within the last decade. They criticized the architecture revealed in the plans. It was too modern looking. Hart wondered if "modern" still referred to a certain style, or if it referred to what was current, and what was modern inevitably became old-fashioned. He found it to be a nice building, as drawn, and that the developers had done a fine job accounting for all the possibilities concerning traffic, parking, and viewsheds. He could see himself living there. He liked the idea of not having to drive. He liked the idea of all the old people around him not driving. Maybe if he was more their age, he would feel more like them. Maybe the plans spooked them. Whatever the reason, the furious conga line of elderly frustration rolled on.

Eventually Hart had a hard time containing his own frustration with those who seemed hardwired for anger. His head rolls and sighs increased. During an especially pronounced look to the ceiling, he dropped his head to one side, hoping to catch a sympathetic glance from the woman in the side aisle seat who wasn't that much younger than him, but younger nonetheless.

He succeeded. She grinned at him in approval of his disapproval. He air-chuckled back and made a chattering mouth with his hand, adding an angry look on his face to give life to his hand puppet.

A small clamor broke out around her. Hart clenched up. He was afraid someone had seen his act and was rallying others to be upset with him. But no one looked his way. Instead they were drawn to the back of the room.

A man who looked like the volunteer assistant coach for every youth football team he had ever played on stood at attention, an assault rifle slung over his shoulder. Hart didn't get a good look at it, but assumed it was an AR-15. He swiveled his head to face the front to see if the council members had caught on.

Someone from the audience, who had recently finished her rant against the permit, approached the bailiff and pointed back toward the man with the gun. Hart checked the armed man's reaction. He was sticking with his impersonation of a palace guard. Hart glanced in the direction of the woman with whom he may have been flirting. She dropped her mouth into an exaggerated expression of concern. Hart acknowledged her and watched the bailiff approach the man, who noticed the bailiff coming and launched into a speech.

"I am within my legal rights to carry this firearm openly on my person," he announced to all. "I have a permit from the county sheriff stating I can lawfully enter any public building, including those times when public hearings are being held. I am exercising first amendment rights in assembling peaceably, and second amendment rights in bearing arms."

The bailiff reached him and spoke softly.

A council member spoke into her microphone.

"Is there an item on this evening's agenda that prompted you to bring a gun?"

"I am not in violation of any law."

"We heard you," the councilwoman said. "But are your actions relevant to something up for discussion tonight?"

"My decision to wear a firearm is no different from someone wearing a hat or a jacket that brings them comfort. Did you bring a purse tonight, Madame Councilwoman?"

Another council member leaned into his microphone.

"Are you really comparing brandishing a gun to wearing a hat?"

"I am not brandishing my weapon, sir. My actions tonight are no more controversial than those of anyone else in this room. To claim otherwise is fear-mongering in the interest of furthering your agenda of disarming the public you claim to serve."

"The second amendment is not the purview of this council," the councilwoman chimed back in. "But we can ask you to leave without violating that amendment. Nor the first amendment, for that matter. Bailiff, will you please escort this man out?"

"On what charge?" the man asked.

"You are causing a disturbance and preventing this body from conducting its business."

"I was assembling peaceably!" he bellowed. "You ordered law enforcement to harass me!"

The bailiff tried to speak to the man again.

The councilman rejoined the fray, grabbing his microphone as though he wished it was the armed man's neck.

"An audience member alerted us," he said. "And several other attendees were visibly concerned by your presence."

Hart tried not to laugh. He was amused at how hard everyone was trying to sound official and dramatic when clearly all they wanted to say to each other was "Fuck you!" "No, fuck you!"

"You cloak your disdain for the second amendment in trumped-up charges!" the man hollered as the bailiff gently took hold of his forearm. "And law enforcement does your bidding so they can take advantage of an unarmed citizenry! We are the true patriots! You are the traitors!"

He swatted away the bailiff's hand. Hart was impressed by the old officer's restraint.

"You're all in on it!" he pointed at the council members and waved his arm back and forth, then started to walk backwards toward the exit.

"There was no school shooting!" he yelled.

Hart felt a paralyzing rush of adrenalin flood his body.

"It was staged by cops under orders from the Department of Homeland Security with crisis actors paid by the federal government! Don't believe the mainstream media! Children are not dying! Your liberty is dying!"

He completed his slow, loud walk to the exit with the bailiff trailing behind.

The woman in the near distance made some kind of face at Hart again, but he was incapable of seeing clearly or registering anything at that moment other than the armed man's affront to law enforcement, dead children, and their families. He was familiar with this derailed train of thought. Groups of its riders had been gathering in front of his daughter's house daily since his grandson ceased living there, inventing evidence to keep the temperature raised on their fever. Hart had been able to take comfort in thinking it was contained, a tight circle under self-inflicted quarantine. Hearing it in a respectable public forum felt like a contagion had been released, a vile of their vitriol shattered, hissing into the air seeking infection. He wanted to follow him out and confront him, but managed to restrain himself. He recalled the cool-down techniques one of his sergeants used to promote. But the accusations and lies spat out by the self-proclaimed patriot at the door were much more personal than what used to happen on the job. People would call him a pig and scream about how much they hate cops, but it was about the uniform. And they never invoked vast, complex conspiracies about that uniform. Occasional accusations about quotas or racism, but never anything as outlandish as what was in the monologue memorized and performed by the armed man.

The ability of any police department to pull off such a lavish plan is giving us way too much credit, Hart thought. The idea that enough people he used to work with could come together in so lockstep a manner was absurd. Some would want more credit than they were due to receive, some more money, others more power. The only issue he could imagine them banding together around would be resisting those kinds of orders from a federal agency. They would crawl over each other to be the first one to blow the whistle on the feds. He was nearing laughter as he considered the logistics of such a plot.

But when the laughter came close, he thought of Stanley, and how that son of a bitch with fake manhood dangling from his shoulder denied that the greatest little grandson who ever lived was dead, and had watched his friends die.

Hart had grown tired of angry people saying that something made their "blood boil." Whatever power the words once had were denuded from overuse, particularly on social media. Whenever someone expressed outrage over a news item, it seemed, that was what they said. "This makes my blood boil."

Now Hart could feel it. His nerves felt like open flames heating his blood. When Stanley's school had been attacked, and the news trickled in and blew up their lives, Hart was too crushed to feel anger that reached very high on the rage scale. Anger was part of the ensuing days, but sadness always prevailed. It was a downpour that doused any flames.

But the denial of the armed man had parted the clouds and lit the fire. Hart didn't even notice when the meeting was adjourned. He didn't know how much time had passed since it had ended, nor how much longer the meeting went on after the disturbance. He saw people milling around and the council seats were empty. Everyone was up and out of their seats except for him. The discovery yanked him out of his thoughts and dropped him in the present. He stood up and found his way to the door.

Once outside, he saw the homemade patriot standing at the threshold of the parking lot. He was standing at attention again, guarding against fears he wanted others to share.

Hart paused to take a deep breath and map a course that veered as far away from the man as possible. A female voice pierced his efforts.

"I know I feel a lot safer," it said.

He turned to find the woman from across the crowded room.

"It's good to know men like him are out there watching out for us," she added with a smirk.

"Yeah," was all Hart could manage.

"If the sheriff really gave that man a permit, I don't think he'll be running unopposed in the next election."

Hart almost said "yeah" again, but caught himself.

Nothing else sprung to mind. He tried to laugh, but could only take another deep breath.

"I'm Peaches," the woman held out her hand.

Hart was temporarily liberated from the one-man show playing in the corner of his eye.

"You're kidding."

"No, really," she smiled.

"I'm sorry."

"I'm used to it."

"I mean I'm sorry for my reaction," he clarified. "Your name is great."

"It was my grandma's nickname. My mom decided to make it legal."

"Sorry for my reactions in general. I'm a little off tonight."

"You're not the only one," she gestured toward the gun slinger.

Hart wasn't ready to laugh about him. His nervous system lit up again. He smiled, but it didn't turn out well. He was relieved when she suggested they get coffee sometime.

"I'd like that," he said, hoping to convey how much he truly meant it.

"What's your number?" she took out her phone.

He recited the digits.

"And what name should I file this under?" she asked.

"Oh. Yes. Of course. Hart."

She tapped the screen.

"A-R-T, I assume?"

"No 'e' in my Hart," he confirmed.

"Got it, Hart. I'd give you my number, but you're acting rather strange."

He laughed, loud enough to make her joke about his behavior seem like a sincere assessment.

"Good God," Hart caught himself. "I'm sorry. It feels so damn good to laugh."

"I've got a million of 'em," Peaches smiled.

He smiled back.

"Thanks for giving a guy a chance."

They shook hands.

"See you, Hart," she said as she walked away.

He watched her go, feeling excited about the possibilities. Extending the moment as long as he could, he waved to her as she drove off before facing the area filled by the volunteer armed guard.

The guardian was being confronted by a man who looked like he had rolled out of bed to teach a geometry class and got lost on the way.

"You don't want to protect a damn thing!" the gun-hating protester yelled at the gun-loving protester. "All you really want to do is roam the streets like some video game and shoot anyone you don't like!"

"If that's the world you fear," the gun-slinger dropped his stoicism. "Then stop trying to disarm responsible gun owners."

"Is this what you call responsible gun ownership?"

"You're the problem, not me. You're in dereliction of duty. If you're not fighting tyranny, you're subject to tyranny."

"Oh, get off script already. More guns, more gun violence. It's that simple."

The people remaining in front of the building and in the parking lot stopped what they were doing but pretended to keep doing them, cell phones ready to capture the moment when the gun was fired.

The two men ran out of talking points and lapsed into screaming insults.

Hart intervened. He walked over and inserted himself between them.

"I don't think we're solving this tonight, gentlemen."

"A gun doesn't solve anything!"

"Sir," Hart directed his attention to the unarmed one, "let's not prove your point by letting this escalate."

"I did not threaten this man!" the armed one said. "He accosted me!"

"I understand," Hart found his old rhythm. "Nobody is saying you did."

"It wouldn't take much, though, would it?" yelled the unarmed one.

"Sir," Hart focused on him, as he seemed to be farther away from calming down, "Let's all get home safe tonight. Back to the people we love, the people who love us."

"I just wanted to go to a fucking city council meeting."

"I know, I know," Hart kept his focus.

"This is bullshit."

"I hear you."

The unarmed man was settling down.

"I don't want to live in that world."

"Nobody does, sir."

"Then don't try to..." the armed man started to speak.

Hart turned and scowled at him.

He stopped.

Hart made sure he was going to stay quiet before turning back to the one without the gun.

"You can have the last word," he assured the unarmed man. "Isn't that right?"

Hart looked back at the armed man, who shrugged.

The unarmed man worked harder to think of something to say now that he was granted the spotlight.

"Would you trust me with a gun?" he finally asked the armed one.

Hart sighed.

"You had to ask a question…"

The armed man puffed back up.

"It's not about trust, it's about freedom," he said, which is pretty much what Hart figured he would say.

"Hoo boy," Hart placed himself in front of the unarmed one.

"Freedom to shoot whoever you want with no consequences," the disheveled one said, his voice starting to rise again.

Hart walked him away from the armed man, who held his ground, as Hart assumed he would.

The unarmed man, meanwhile, seemed satisfied with his last statement, as though it was what he wished he had said the first time he was granted the last word. Or maybe he was tired. He stopped backing up and turned to walk to his car with no need of an escort. Hart kept an eye on him to make sure. The man climbed into his car and drove out of the lot at a more reasonable speed than Hart expected.

The armed man resumed his guard stance, probably to prove how responsible and reasonable he was compared to his foe.

Hart lingered a while to make sure the unarmed one didn't simply take a lap around the block and return, perhaps armed. The audience members who also lingered realized there would be nothing worth recording, and slunk away.

The lot was practically empty by the time Hart decided to join the exodus. He wanted to leave before the bailiff or council members came out. He pretended the armed man wasn't there. But he refused to be ignored.

"You law enforcement?" he called over.

"Retired," Hart answered in stride.

"Oath Keeper?"

Hart had heard rumors of colleagues who considered themselves part of that group. As suspicious as he had been of certain people in his profession, he never took it that far, in large part because some of those he was most suspicious of had taken the oath. It seemed like they used it as an excuse to never be off duty.

He shook his head.

The man walked toward him.

Hart thought maybe he didn't see him shake his head.

"I said no."

The man stopped.

"Sorry, dude. You just seemed like one of the cool ones."

Then he smiled.

Hart took a few steps in his direction.

"What makes you think I'm on your side?"

"You weren't distracted by the gun. You could see who was causing the problem."

"That was the situation. Don't read too much into it."

"Come on," the man came a little closer and extended his hand. "I know a patriot when I see one. I'm Glenn."

Hart stayed back.

"You really think the school shooting was a hoax?"

Glenn lowered his hand.

"You don't?"

"I know people whose children died."

"They're in on it."

"They identified the bodies."

"So they say."

"Where are their children?"

"Somewhere else," he brushed off the question. "All expenses paid."

Hart caught his breath and thought of ways to keep from hitting him.

"Fascinating," he decided to say, because it was fascinating in its own weird right, and because the word made it look like he was pondering the merits of Glenn's idea, rather than ways to kill him.

"It is, isn't it?" Glenn was excited at the prospect of converting someone.

Hart looked for cameras on the building and on the light posts in the parking lot. He saw none, but assumed more people would be on their way out soon, the council members, bailiff, and those who had stuck around to pester them.

"I'd like to hear more," Hart said. "Why don't you meet me at the Applebee's by the freeway? I'll buy you a beer."

"Awesome."

"I'm BC, by the way," Hart finally took up Glenn on his handshake.

"Great to meet you, BC."

"See you there in ten minutes."

Hart let him get a head start.

He hoped the drive would give him a chance to reconsider, to let the fire run its course. But it only raged higher and jumped to parts of his body he didn't know were capable of anger. His joints ached.

He reached an intersection that offered a chance to turn toward his neighborhood before the street he was on became the frontage road where Applebee's stood beside the other franchises. He swiped on his turn signal, trying to force himself to heed the call of the blinking light on the dashboard. After a brief staring contest between him and the little green arrow, he looked away, turned it off, and proceeded through the crossroads.

Glenn was waiting in front, pacing the walkway unarmed. There was still a chance this wouldn't happen. Hart left it up to fate.

"Aren't you going to wear your gun?" he asked as he stepped up onto the curb with him.

Glenn grinned and went to retrieve it. He headed for the lot that was around the back of the restaurant. Hart had his answer.

"So be it," he thought to himself.

He followed Glenn to his car and stood quietly behind him as he fetched his rifle from the backseat floor. Glenn didn't know he was there. He stood up, shut the door, and was about to sling the rifle over his shoulder as he turned around. He cut the action short and still had a grip on the gun as he stood face-to-face with Hart.

Glenn was startled, but laughed it off.

"What's up?" he asked.

He held the rifle in front of him, but was unable to raise it since Hart was so close.

"I'm giving you one last chance," Hart said. "If that wasn't my grandson's body I identified at the coroner's office, whose body was it?"

Glenn stared at him and figured something out. Disbelief turned into a sneer.

"You're one of them," he started to let out a dismissive snort.

Hart punched him before he could finish.

The head snapped to and fro. Hart couldn't read the face. It was in ruins. The legs pedaled backward at the same time they went slack, giving way by the third step. Once the body had tumbled to the ground, on its back, the remaining air inside bubbled up through the leftovers of the nose.

Hart stood over him and wondered if that was his last breath.

If Glenn wasn't done, he wondered if he would finish him, or if he would take advantage of the chance to save him.

No choice presented itself. No breath came.

Glenn had not let go of his gun. It was in his dead hand, which would soon be cold.

Voices came from the front of the restaurant.

Hart crouched down beside the body. It would serve him right to get caught. He considered standing up and surrendering. Maybe claim self-defense. Maybe tell the truth. The voices drew closer.

He wasn't ready to make that decision. He called on fate again.

His interpretation of the events was going to matter more than what happened. If he got away with it, that could mean he was lucky and he'd never do it again. Or maybe it was an invitation, a sign that his mission had begun.

He looked over Glenn's body and under his car. Four pairs of feet walked between the cars one spot over. They proceeded to walk farther into the lot and engage in some small talk.

More voices emerged from the restaurant, but they went straight ahead into the spaces in front of the building.

The double date who almost stumbled upon him wrapped things up and said their goodnights.

"Let's do this again sometime," a man said.

The couples climbed into their cars and drove off. Each driver had a chance to spot Hart if they happened to look over as they passed by, but neither did.

CHAPTER 4

"Armed Man Found Punched to Death" was the headline in the local paper. The article on their website received more hits than all the other articles they had ever published combined. The story was a viral sensation that mainstream media sources dodged. They didn't want to be accused of making fun of a murder victim.

People on social media had no such worries. The jokes and memes were relentless. They came from every direction.

Gun lovers adhered to a "use it or lose it" theme.

Gun loathers gravitated more toward, "The only thing that can stop a bad guy with a gun is a good guy with a gun. The only thing that can stop a good guy with a gun is a fist."

Which implied that Glenn was a good guy. But those on the left did seem to feel more sorry for him than those on the right, who countered with "Facing a Left jab? Give them a Right hook," with a picture of a gun representing the right hook.

Hart fell ill for several days afterwards, unable to take his neighborhood walks with Nando, or his solo treks downtown. His head felt bloated, his muscles weak, like a cold and a flu were battling each other to a standstill over the rights to his body.

He would watch his six seconds of Stanley to try and rationalize what he did.

A bruise ran across his knuckles. He wrapped his hand in a bandage so he wouldn't have to look at it. He would check it once a day, late at night when he moved from his couch to his bed. It marked his time. As the bruise faded, his health returned. When he no longer needed to hide it, he no longer needed to hide from the world.

To give himself a final checkup, he went to the police station.

He was more interested in Glenn than anything else. He wondered who this man was he had killed. Hart had never killed anyone on the job. He had rarely drawn his weapon over his twenty-five years. Now in retirement, he had murdered someone with his bare hands. Someone whose only crime was idiocy.

"Nobody seems to have known the guy," said the officer in charge of the case. "A real loner."

"Family?" Hart asked, adopting the clipped tone of his days on the investigator's side of the desk.

"A mother in a convalescent hospital a couple hours away."

"Nobody who's going to put any pressure on you, then."

"Nope," the officer looked relieved. "We were thinking some of his gun club buddies could get pushy, but they're all online, none of them local."

"What about that cult taking videos of the school families?"

"They want nothing to do with him, either. He's not exactly the ideal martyr for the cause. Maybe if he'd gone down with his gun blazing."

"I'm surprised the gun was still on him."

"Me, too. When I first heard about it, I thought for sure it was a gun deal gone bad. But not only was his AR-15 on him, he had a whole stack of weapons in the trunk left untouched. All different kinds."

"Maybe there were some select items stolen."

"The trunk was never opened," the officer shook his head. "If it was a deal, the customer never even saw the merchandise. As far as we can tell, our boy must have really pissed someone off. Simple as that."

Hart nodded and searched the officer for signs of anything being implied by his statement. But it had been clear to Hart from the moment he walked in that he was not a suspect.

"I know there's only so much you can share about the case…"

The officer waved him off.

"You're family," he said. "Besides, I don't think I'm giving away any secrets in saying we've got nothing."

"What about the man he had the verbal confrontation with?"

"Verified alibi. Went home afterwards. Stopped by the grocery store on the way. So we've got video, not just family."

"Anyone else from the council meeting?"

"Technically everyone, present company excluded. But most of them are a bit too frail to deliver that kind of blow."

"That narrows it down."

"If the council meeting was an isolated incident. He and his gun were on tour. We found a paper trail of complaints against him."

"Oops."

"Oops is right. We're screwed."

"Sorry."

"At least nobody cares," the officer said. "We've got that going for us."

Hart felt worse than if Glenn had been an upstanding member of the community. He felt like a bully, picking on the unnerving kid that even the most compassionate classmate would have a hard time standing up for.

"I should have come by earlier," Hart buried his guilt in an apology. "I didn't want to impose."

"Don't worry about it."

"It's bad enough I butted in that night, like some ex-cop who can't move on."

"You did the right thing," the officer assured him. "It's who you are."

It's who you are.

The words shadowed him.

"Have you heard of these groups who think mass shootings are staged?" he asked Nando one morning after he had started to walk again.

He would have started walking even if he was still feeling ill. Spending time in the house brought on an eerie feeling. He'd sit there consciously aware of how much time there is to fill in a life, unsure whether it was a lot of time, or a little.

"Of course," Nando said. "Why?"

"They guy who got punched was screaming about it at the council meeting."

Nando chuckled.

"What?" Hart asked. He expected to hear another joke about Glenn.

"Still cracks me up that you went to a city council meeting."

"It wasn't dull."

"You caught one on a good night."

"Seriously?"

"That guy was an embarrassment to gun owners everywhere."

"So good riddance?"

"He accomplished a lot more by dying the way he did than his little crusade was ever going to manage."

"How not to be a gun advocate," Hart confirmed.

"Thank you, Glenn. Rest in peace."

They huffed along for a short while.

"So what's next?' Nando asked. "Water aerobics? Bingo?"

Hart laughed and told him to fuck off.

They walked in relative quiet for the remainder of that walk, and the walks they took in the proceeding days. They avoided the subject of guns. It was important to Hart that he was able to remain friends with someone who disagreed with him. He needed to spend time with a person who saw the world from a different perspective and not kill them. He wasn't sure what Nando's reasons were for avoiding the subject. Maybe because whenever the topic came up, people wanted to talk about Glenn.

Someone finally got around to posting his obituary. Perhaps his mother. Whomever it was, they also avoided mentioning guns, for obvious reasons. But that didn't leave them much to work with. He had a dog that he rescued. He visited his mother. He liked to drive. There was no memorial service. Donations would be accepted in his name to the animal shelter.

Hart invited Nando on his downtown route.

He wished he hadn't.

Nando didn't handle himself well in the coffee house where Hart enjoyed spending time before he would reverse course and walk back home. It had hip ambitions to be like the coffee houses in the big cities, and Nando liked to loudly make fun of them for it. He would make snide remarks about the men with big, rustic beards and clean, skinny fingers, and about the tattooed young ladies who worked the counter. Hart felt like an adolescent trapped in a public place with a proudly out-of-touch father, cringing at his dad's volume.

He kept inviting him, though. He figured the humiliation was well-deserved, and it kept his memories away from the bloody wetlands he made of Glenn's face. He wished he could use Nando's jokes as a diversion in the way they were intended, but he was having a hard time laughing at people.

"Aw, come on," Nando chided him. "These peacocks see you the same way they see me."

"But they can also hear you," Hart muttered.

As if to further enhance the feeling of being the younger, embarrassed end of a father-son relationship, Peaches came in one morning as they sat in the corner. The girl who never called. He wished there was a deeper corner he could sink into.

Nando caught his expression.

"What?" he followed Hart's line of sight.

"Don't look," Hart pleaded. "Please don't..."

But she saw them. Hart wasn't sure how to read the smile she flashed before turning to place her order.

"Who's that?" Nando asked in a way that led Hart to believe he had picked up on the dad dynamic and was going with it.

"I met her at the city council meeting."

"She must be older than she looks."

"I don't know. I barely talked to her."

Peaches walked over.

"Hello, mystery man."

"Hi, Peaches."

"Peaches?" Nando blurted.

"Have we met?" she extended her hand to him.

"Nando," he took it. "You a nurse?"

Hart hadn't even noticed that she was wearing medical scrubs.

"I'm a doctor," she said as they finished their shake.

"Really?" he looked over at Hart. "What kind?"

"Geriatrics."

"You chose the right town," Nando cackled. "Lots of old farts around here."

"Uh oh," she smirked. "I'm supposed to be semi-retired. Taking it easy."

"Not that we know any," Hart joined in.

"Not that I could call you to find out," she quipped.

Her tone smacked Hart with a realization.

"Dammit," he tossed his head back. "I'm sorry. Swedish massage?"

"Yes," her smirk warmed up into a smile.

"That's the number I used to give out when I was a cop."

"Give out to whom?" she asked. "Drug dealers? Bag men?"

"Hookers?" Nando added.

Hart and Peaches glanced at him.

"I bring him along to make me look good," Hart explained.

"You need more than that," Nando shot back.

He ignored Nando and focused on Peaches.

"That number is just an old habit," Hart told her. "I was a little cautious back then."

"Back then," she nodded slowly. "You married?"

Nando scoffed.

"Geez," Hart glared at him. "Some help you would be if I was."

"I'm too old to be a wing man," he waved him off and turned to Peaches. "He's separated."

"Divorced," Hart corrected him.

"I was giving you options," Nando shrugged.

Peaches reacted in mock offense.

"So do you want to try this again or not?" she asked Hart.

"Now that you know my great track record."

"Of course he wants to," Nando answered on his behalf.

Hart started feeling like the father instead, giving his son a disapproving look.

"You wanted a wing man," Nando defended himself.

Peaches gestured at the two phones on the table.

"One of those yours?" she asked Hart.

"They're both mine," Nando said. "I started a side business in retirement."

"Maybe I should get your number," she said.

"He's married."

"Damn you, Hart!" Nando slapped the table.

Hart picked up his phone.

"Now that you don't need mine as a prop for your crappy jokes."

Nando looked at Peaches and pointed back and forth between himself and Hart.

"See what you've done to us?" he said to her.

"It's always a woman," she shook her head.

"Let's do this," Hart said, raising his phone in anticipation.

Peaches held her phone on her hip as though she was waiting to draw a gun.

"You want to shoot first?" she asked. "Or should I?"

He paused.

"You," he said.

She gave him her number. His finger shook as he tapped it onto the screen. He had to correct himself after almost every digit.

"Long walk and too much coffee," he excused his mistakes.

When it was her turn, she pulled her phone and aimed it at him.

"Tell the truth," she warned him.

He gave her his real number. She typed with her thumbs and seemed to finish before he was done speaking. He was impressed, and told her so, while telling himself that this may be the best way to put what he had done behind him.

CHAPTER 5

He was ashamed of how easy it was to forget his victim. He wanted to attribute as much of his amnesia as possible to Peaches and her wonderfulness. Everything was funny when they were together. She could have told Nando's jokes and he would have laughed. The warm breeze he had felt with his grandson came back with her. The warmth came from a different direction, but it was the first to have passed through him since Stanley's death.

She was a one-person wrecking crew when it came to the cement ego he had constructed over his years as a male in a very male profession. He told her some of the worst things he had encountered on the job, things he had not shared with his wife. He told Peaches about the man in the wheelchair at the bottom of the pool, the bedsores on the four-hundred pound woman locked in the dark bedroom, the dog fight ring, and he wondered if maybe it wasn't so much her, but because enough time had passed that he was so willing to open up. She just happened to be the one who was there when he was ready.

He felt so comfortable around her, that in the odd moments when he did remember Glenn, he had to catch himself from revealing his identity as the infamous thrower of that notorious punch.

"Is Hart short for something?" she asked as they lay on their backs in the middle of his living room floor. It had occurred to them that one of the great things about sex in their station of life is that they didn't have to be confined to the bedroom.

He felt more reticent about revealing his full name than confessing to manslaughter, which made him laugh.

"I didn't start using it until I became a cop."

"That doesn't answer my question."

"It's short for Bernhart."

"Why not go with Bernie?"

"I did when I was a kid."

"Aw. I would feel great knowing Officer Bernie was on the beat."

"Yeah, that's exactly what he sounds like. A fat, old beat cop from the 1950s. I wanted to be a young, badass cop. I thought Hart would lead to some word play. It would be ironic, because I would be so heartless."

"Ooh…" she teased.

"I still kind of used Bernie. It was part of my fake name."

"To go with the fake number?"

"That's right. I was BC."

"What does the 'C' stand for?"

He hesitated before answering.

"Cop."

Peaches rolled over with laughter onto her side, away from Hart.

"So you're Bernie the Cop after all," she managed to say.

"You are in rare company," he playfully smacked her bare ass. "I never tell anyone what it really means. BC is primal, caveman shit."

She farted.

He laughed even harder than she was laughing.

"And here I thought I was going to have to hold that in," she said as they calmed down.

"You're welcome," he said.

"Why didn't you just go with your middle initial."

"My middle name is Fredrick. I couldn't go with BF."

"Why not Fred? Or Rick?"

He stared at the ceiling and thought about it.

"I wanted a fresh start. I wasn't sure I was cut out for police work. Like I wasn't tough enough."

He thought about it a little more.

"Turns out that wasn't a problem."

"It was the job, not you," she assured him. "You had no choice but to grow a thick skin."

"But I took it too far."

"How so?"

He almost told her.

But he didn't do it for her sake. That was his excuse. He didn't want to burden her. When he confessed, he would do so directly to the police.

If he confessed.

He had endured more than his share of pain before he found himself on the floor with such a fantastic woman. And in his bed, and her bed, and his car, and her car, and behind the oak trees on the hiking trail that led up to the highest peak that surrounded the valley. He deserved Peaches. He had put Glenn out of his misery.

"I started to feel like I was always right," he said instead. "I could justify anything."

"You and everyone else."

He looked at her, grateful to be considered part of the human race. They kissed and explored one another again.

There was only one disappointing discovery he made with her, something that revealed more of itself the more they were together.

He couldn't tell her that he loved her. He didn't want her to say anything about love, either. The specter of Peaches saying "I love you" hung over him much more heavily than the memory of the sad, lonely life he took in the parking lot of a family restaurant.

Not that he didn't love her. It wasn't hard to understand, even for someone like him. He had enough memories he could dust off from decades before when he first met his wife. If you thought you loved someone, then you did. But if Peaches loved him as much as he loved her, that meant he wasn't giving off anything that would scare her away. She said she had put up with too many lost causes in her life to put even one more on her back. She could fool around with one, but she wouldn't commit to one. She vowed to fall in love with someone who deserved her.

And if he was the one, that meant he wasn't relying on her to help him forget what he had done. It meant he had a talent for it.

He already suspected as much. Not only was it terribly easy for him to move on from Glenn once the initial shock subsided, but he found himself wanting more. He would gravitate toward stories on the web of Oath Keepers and Three Percenters and various conspiracy groups guided by the same philosophy as Glenn, and a familiar impulse would clutch him. It was as though he had proven himself capable of striking back at them in the only way they may have a chance of understanding, as Quentin had proposed, and he was intrigued with proceeding. In the paranoid circles he stalked, there was much bragging about a willingness to die for their beliefs. He wanted to see if they meant it.

Maybe this was where he could rely on love. If Peaches brought him that close to confessing, then perhaps she could subdue his desire to follow through on Quentin's awful plan. He wondered if the warm breeze generated by Peaches blew stronger than the one blown by the memory of Stanley. He needed to test what was more powerful: his affection for Peaches or his grudge against those who considered his grandson collateral damage in the fight for their rights.

Peaches suggested they take a road trip together.

She also considered it a test.

"We could be in this for the long haul if we make it there and back together," she said.

He agreed, but for different reasons.

And he knew just the place where each of their exams could be administered.

In the course of tracking the sorts of groups with whom Glenn aligned himself, Hart had learned that a town up in the mountains, a few hours out and above the valley, was an unofficial regional headquarters for one of them. It caught his eye because he and his wife used to take Megan there in the winter to go sledding when she was a little girl.

He emphasized the luxury lodge and ski resort within a half hour of the town when he ran it by Peaches, so it didn't sound like an odd suggestion. She liked the idea of getting a dose of snow.

"We'll likely have to drive a couple thousand feet higher before we see any," he said. "The town will probably just be wet and gray."

"Not when I'm with you," she fluttered her eyes.

"The town is for the cheap room. We'll spend the afternoon and evening up at the resort. They've got a great lounge and restaurant."

"Beats staying at the resort and coming down into town to eat at McDonalds."

Plus it allowed him to pay cash for their room.

He also left his phone at home, but that was an easy excuse to compose, a story about wanting to commit to the mountains and leave everyday life behind.

The cash was more challenging. He was prepared to blame his old police habits if she was next to him when they checked in, but Peaches lingered by the brochures in the lobby to search for other attractions in the area.

The woman at the front desk required a different explanation. When Hart brought out the cash, he may as well have offered to pay in beaver pelts. He told her he was trying to straighten out his finances, following the advice of a talk radio money guru by cutting up his credit cards. The story made enough sense to her, and she started the proceedings. As they conducted their business, Hart imagined how his story about being a jumpy ex-cop would have gone over. He smiled and signed in under the name "BC Hart".

Peaches had worked her way down to the bottom rung of the brochures by the time he was done at the front desk.

"Any ideas?" Hart asked as she returned a pamphlet to its slot.

"There's a wine trail nearby."

"What's the wine made from?"

"It's down in the foothills. Some of the wineries in that part of the valley."

"Maybe on the way back, then."

He embraced her and offered to take her bag to their room.

The room was sufficient. Not the type anyone would want to spend much time in, so it was easy enough to convince her to take a walk around town.

In the late afternoon light, it was as gray as he had predicted. They held hands while he scanned the surroundings for the kinds of vehicles driven by the kinds of people he was interested in. He was able to keep the conversation going easily enough, and found what he was looking for just as easily.

He spotted some white pickup trucks marked by "Give Them a Right Hook" bumper stickers. They were in a parking lot in front of a bar that looked like a hangout for people whose neighbors complained about them.

"If we're going to do this town," Hart said. "Let's go native."

He gestured toward the dim box with the neon beer signs that made such small promises. She was game, as he knew she would be.

"We may never make it to the resort," she captioned their view of the bar.

He figured either everyone would look at them when they walked in, or no one would.

No one did.

But that was because no one was there. Technically there were a couple of figures dumped onto stools facing the television, but their consciousness was debatable. Hart was more confused than disappointed. Maybe the two apparitions at the bar would eventually break into heated conversation about government overreach.

"Think they can make something without beer in it?" Peaches asked as they grabbed a table.

"Do you really want to find out?"

"Bud Light. Straight."

"Two fingers?" he asked her as he drifted toward the bartender.

"Just give me the bottle."

"Whoa. You fit right in."

Their affectionate banter helped camouflage his intentions to move on and keep searching for the white pickup party. The bar gave them plenty of material to work with, and a convenient reason to leave after they finished their beers.

When they went back outside, he saw a coffee house across the parking lot that reminded him of the place they met. Peaches noticed it, too.

"Where did people sit and solve the problems of the world before coffee houses?" she asked.

"Bars?"

"That's where they create problems."

Hart chuckled as they passed the pickup trucks on their way past the front window of the coffee house. She slid her arm around his. He tilted his head skyward to take in the feeling, and when he lowered it for a glance into the window, he saw them.

He assumed it was them.

They wore hoodies and mesh baseball caps with gun logos on them. They had laptops spread around the table they shared, propped up among the coffee cups. Their laptops were splattered with decals: Gadsden flags, Free Republic logos, Jerusalem crosses, and drawings of Knights Templar in melodramatic poses that looked like they belonged on a heavy metal album cover thirty years ago rather than a battlefield one thousand years ago.

"Of course," Hart said aloud.

"Of course what?"

"Oh," he mentally scurried to cover his tracks. "Maybe if old bars like the one we just haunted offered free Wi-Fi, they'd keep up."

"You think people who dive into a place like that are interested in staying connected to the world?"

He laughed at how ill-conceived his cover was, and how unnecessary. Peaches had no reason to believe he was doing anything other than enjoying her company, because it was so easy to do.

After a lap around town, they retired to their room before dinner. They made love and used each other for pillows afterwards, congratulating themselves on their ability to make sex better each time they had it.

"There has to be a ceiling," she speculated. "A limit."

"If we find it, we'll move laterally. Take things in a new direction."

They silently relished the thought.

Hart's silence was invaded by visions of the hoodies and laptops in the coffee house. He wondered if they were still there.

"I need a jolt," he said. "Otherwise I might fall asleep at dinner."

"Old man."

He extracted himself from her.

"With enough caffeine I can shave off a good ten years. Want anything from that coffee house we passed?"

"I'm fine," she said, loaded with implications.

While he got dressed, she reached for the remote and turned on the television. She settled on a station by the time he finished.

"The Food Network," he noticed. "And I'm the old one?"

"Yes," she squeezed in before he kissed her.

"I'll be back," he said as he headed for the door.

"Don't be too long," she called after him. "We want to catch the early bird special."

It was a slow time of day for a coffee house. The place was half empty, but there was still a foursome of them huddled around the same table strewn with laptops and cups. The membership appeared to have changed slightly. Some had left and been replaced by others. This was good news to Hart. They were a reliable presence.

Hart ordered a coffee and made eye contact with one of them. They were all young, but this one appeared to be the youngest. His goatee was surrounded by razor burn.

Hart nodded approvingly.

The young man nodded back, the edges of his goatee lifted by his smile.

Upon receiving his order, Hart sat at the table next to them. They were half his age and from a very different domain, but joining in the conversation was easy. He had scoured enough websites and followed their comment threads. When putting forward an idea, he made sure to use the words "liberty" and "freedom", and the phrase "Founding Fathers". When putting down an idea, he went with "socialist", "globalist", and "politically correct". He tried to sound like his words were written in calligraphy, as though he was addressing a crowd rather than a person.

Their talk remained rather standard for a while, boiler plate issues, some of which he agreed with. Subjugation, betrayal, infringement, all thanks to a lack of personal responsibility enabled by the federal government. When the members started in on race, and used words like "degradation" and "dilution" with no concern over offending him, he knew he had gained their trust. He was safe.

Since he passed their test, he could start his.

He brought up school shootings.

"It's sad what happened to those kids," he forced himself to say. "But we can't let that infringe on our liberty."

One of them pounced, the one with the fullest beard.

"Nothing happened to any kids."

The one with a more trimmed beard shook his head, while the goateed member exhaled. Meanwhile, the one whose beard grew in patches addressed the situation.

"C'mon, Wade," he said. "Do we have to go through this again?"

"Nothing to go through," said Wade. "If you can't see it by now, I ain't wasting my breath."

"It's tough to break up the marriage between a person and their point," Hart tried to sympathize with everyone at the table.

"You make us look bad with that shit," the one with the patchy beard would not be appeased.

"We're not saying it's not part of the agenda," said the trimmed beard, as much for Hart's sake as for Wade's. "But there's a more reasonable version."

"And that's all it is," Wade shook his head. "A version. You're still saying it's rigged, but you ain't willing to go all the way. So you come up with this middle-of-the-road bullshit. It's like you're running for office. You really think anyone joins us for moderation?"

"It's not just about our team," the trimmed beard maintained his lead on behalf of the rest of them. "It's about being a legitimate voice, being taken seriously."

"So what's this middle-of-the-road position?" Hart asked.

"Get on the site, man," the patchy beard jumped back in. "Show him the home page, Johnny."

The goateed one took his cue and spun his laptop toward Hart.

Hart leaned in to the screen. Below an eagle, in the middle of some white pillars, it read "Sons of Liberty".

"That name wasn't taken?" Hart asked.

"It may be," Johnny said. "But if we get a leg up on the others, it won't matter."

"We're a splinter of a splinter group," Wade kept tormenting them.

Johnny ignored him.

"We're trying to package our ideas in a more appealing way," he pitched to Hart.

"Sellouts," Wade muttered.

Johnny worked harder to ignore him.

"If the federal government can fool people into buying their ideas..."

"They have to disguise theirs!" Wade grew more agitated. "They're peddling slavery. We're offering freedom."

"It's all about power," Johnny maintained.

"Then you're no better than them," Wade said, then appeared to be finished for the night. He folded his arms and sat back.

The other three exchanged looks and sighed.

The table had reached a stalemate.

"So..." Hart resubmitted his question to anyone who was willing to break the silence. "The school shootings?"

"Randy? Chad?" Johnny asked his allies. "A little help? Wade got me off my game. I need some time."

"Well," Randy took the job, and stroked his neatly-cropped beard as if it helped him find the right words. "The shootings are real. But the cops let it happen."

"Like 9/11," Chad chipped in. "Some say Bush and his cronies were responsible. That's giving the feds way too much credit. The more reasonable explanation is they let it happen. It just makes sense. The federal government can't do anything right, but they can sit and do nothing just fine."

"Ah," Hart nodded to keep himself calm. "Then if it happens often enough, the cops get our guns."

"They're practically encouraging it," Johnny got his game back.

"But the cops and the schools are part of the same community," Hart said. "Wouldn't some of the cops have kids in the school getting shot up?"

"Possibly," Randy acknowledged. "But they have ways of keeping their kids safe."

"How?" Hart was genuinely intrigued.

"Which schools they patrol, first of all," Randy held on as chief spokesperson for the conspiracy. "They maintain more of a presence at their own kids' schools. Park near the crosswalks in the morning to make it look like they're helping out the crossing guards. Drop in more frequently during the day. Shooters are looking for soft targets. They go for the school that doesn't seem to have so many cops hovering over it."

"And even if that doesn't work," Chad added. "Even if the shooter didn't notice the patrols, or ignored them for whatever reason, most of the kids are going to survive. Let's say you've got a couple hundred kids at the school. A big number is twenty victims, right? That's huge. That's still only ten percent of the school. And that's a small school with a high body count. Most shootings are only going to take out five percent or less. That's a ninety-five percent survival rate. And it happens maybe once or twice a year."

"We're supposed to burn the Constitution over this?" Johnny asked hypothetically while looking at Hart.

They all looked at Hart, as if for approval.

He couldn't quite bring himself to pretend to offer it. But he wanted to maintain their bond. He hid behind another question.

"You think cops are willing to take even a fraction of a chance with their kids' lives?" he asked with a sneer he hoped they would interpret as being condescending to the police, as though they didn't have the grit.

"They win no matter what," Randy said. "Even if the shooter beats the odds, it helps the cause. Some things are bigger than the individual."

"You're not giving cops enough credit," said Chad.

"I'm not?"

"Never underestimate your enemy," Chad explained. "We're willing to sacrifice ourselves for what we believe. We should assume they're just as strong in their beliefs."

Their scheme was the most backhanded compliment to law enforcement Hart could fancy, as though the hand that delivered it had been amputated, and was being used as a prop by another hand that was still attached.

"What about your families?" Hart asked.

"What about them?"

"You said you're willing to sacrifice yourselves. But the cops are sacrificing their families. Isn't that harder?"

"You saw the name," Johnny said. "We're the sons. We are the family that our fathers are willing to sacrifice."

"No children of your own?"

"Not until we clean up this world," Randy answered.

"Except for Wade," cracked Chad. "He'd start a family, but he can't get laid."

Wade tried to shoot back at Chad with a remark about his blotchy beard, and how he couldn't even clean that up, but eventually laughed at himself along with the rest of them.

Hart thought it best to leave on a high note, telling them he had to get back to his woman, and rolling with the teasing they lobbed at him about being whipped.

"I'm not gonna lie to you, boys," he teased back. "If you find a good woman, the revolution is over."

He clasped each of their hands, fist bumped, and exchanged pleasantries. He gave them one more wave on his way past the window, feeling pretty certain he had made it through the obstacle course.

Dinner with Peaches, and a full day in her company, had him fully convinced he was beyond the reach of Quentin's horrible idea, and the excuse it provided for his own vicious fantasies.

They spent one more night in their cheap hotel after a day of poaching the amenities of the five-star resort up the mountain, engulfed by the views of clean snow, accompanied by haute cuisine and premium liquor. He barely thought of the Sons of Liberty and their loony hypothesis. When he did, he laughed them off, the latest in a line of contented noises he couldn't help but make in her presence.

Peaches had won. The points he had made in favor of Quentin's stance would stop at one. Maybe that was enough. Maybe Glenn's story convinced a few people to play the odds and disarm. He had seen a sticker that read "Mo' Guns, Mo' Problems" and thought perhaps it was inspired by what he had done. He looked it up and discovered the phrase had predated his action. But maybe that sticker had sold better since then.

They veered onto the wine trail on their way down the mountain, stopping at one with a familiar label, and another they had never heard of.

The unknown got their vote. Everything they sipped had an aggressive flavor they liked.

"Maybe it's our amateur palates," Peaches said. "We don't know any better."

"Maybe it took us by surprise, and when we drink it at home, we'll realize our mistake."

"So you're buying me a bottle?"

"I'm buying you a case."

He didn't have enough cash, but was confident their trip had put Quentin's idea to rest. He slapped his debit card onto the counter.

She reciprocated with a couple bottles of her own for him, which were placed in the kind of fashionable gift bag he thought had disappeared from his life.

The adorable bag of wine was the first thing he brought inside when he arrived home.

His phone was on the kitchen counter. He checked it before heading back out the car.

As expected, there was a text from Peaches that she sent right after he dropped her off.

"Admit it," she wrote. "U left ur phone behind on accident, not on purpose, old man."

He wrote back.

"If I'm old, what does that make u?"

Seconds later, she responded.

"Very happy."

He smiled, then another message from her popped onscreen.

"Now leave me alone. I need to get some rest."

He wished her sweet dreams and checked his other texts.

There was one from Nando asking if Hart would be back in time for a walk the next day, and a collection from Megan.

"Where are you?" she asked every time.

She was fastidious when it came to her texts. She always wrote out whole words, never succumbing to maneuvers like writing "u" instead of "you".

"Roadie with new lady friend," he sent back. "Left my phone behind. Sorry."

He adhered to her rules when texting with her.

Her phone was always on due to her work, so it came as no surprise when he saw that she was responding right away.

"So you're back?"

"Just got in."

"Can you stop by?"

"Sure. Everything OK?"

He wondered if it was okay to write "OK" instead of "okay".

"Nothing urgent. Just want to talk."

She hadn't expressed interest in talking to him for quite some time. He said he would be right over. Nothing urgent? To her, maybe.

To him, it was yet another gift. He went back out to the car and didn't bother bringing his travel bag into the house.

He not only had romance, he had a daughter who loved him.

Having such strong relationships with the women in his life confirmed the results of his mountain run. They would never love a monster.

CHAPTER 6

After several hours on the road, Hart would have liked to walk to Megan's house. It was only about a mile outside the city limits that bordered his neighborhood. But the country roads had no sidewalks, and the vehicles drove them at highway speeds.

The home had a driveway that was a road of its own, running a half mile from the street to the house. A sunburned pair of white-haired people turned out to be a man and a woman as he decelerated toward their spot where the private road met the public. They could have been mistaken for a homeless couple shuffling along the shoulder if not for the camera phones they held up as he made the turn.

"Tell Megan she can run but she can't hide!" the man shouted as he shoved the camera within inches of the glass.

"Say hi to Stanley for us!" added the woman, also recording the moment.

Hart ignored them and proceeded toward his daughter's house.

He passed the herd of goats fenced in along the right side. They were down to three, from the original seven they had collected by the time Stanley had grown from a baby to a toddler. After Stanley died, Megan and Quentin stopped replenishing them. When a goat died, it meant one less. The diminishing herd mirrored the condition of the house. It looked good from a distance, but up close, the need for some patchwork, paint, and weeding was apparent. They both traveled a lot now, and neither was interested in entertaining.

Megan answered the door and also seemed to have withered from the last time he saw her, which was only a matter of weeks. The look in her eyes was even more pronounced, the look of someone about to scream at something that isn't there. She appeared to be seeing something even farther away than before.

He gave her a peck on the cheek while they said their hellos.

"Small crowd today," he nodded back toward the road.

"They work in shifts now," she shrugged. "Did they shoot video of you?"

"Yes."

She sighed and stood to the side.

"Breaking news," she followed him in. "They're going to say Stanley was in the trunk. The only question is whether you were smuggling him in, or smuggling him out."

He turned into the living room and took a seat on the couch that faced the panoramic window with a view of the countryside. The hills and glades were green from the winter rain, with patches of wildflowers starting to emerge, some yellow, some purple. An occasional oak tree was a reminder of where everything had been, and where it was all headed, their twisted branches still leafless and reaching for light in every direction. The window frame may as well have been a picture frame.

She sat down on the couch opposite him, her back to the beauty.

"Guess where I was with my new squeeze?" he forced a change of subject.

"Your squeeze?"

"I don't know what to call a girlfriend at my age. 'Girlfriend' sounds so juvenile."

"As opposed to squeeze?"

"We figure the more blatantly immature, the better the term for us."

"We? Us? Sounds promising."

"Oh, it is. And guess where we were?"

"I hate when people ask that. I don't know. Tokyo? Istanbul?"

"Come on. Driving distance."

"Fuck. The Grand Canyon? Yellowstone?"

"Remember where Mom and I used to take you sledding?"

"Yes. And if I remember correctly, snow is all it has to offer."

"Got a resort there now. Well, up the hill a ways. You should meet her. Let's double date, if you and Quentin are ever in town at the same time. Where is he now? Palo Alto? Bangalore?"

"Guangdong Province."

"My next guess. So what's up?"

She took a deep breath.

"I'm pregnant," she exhaled.

"Holy shit!" Hart raised his arms. "That's great!"

She smiled just enough to prove she had smiled.

"What?" he lowered his arms and expectations. "It's not Quentin's?"

"Oh, please," Megan waved him off. "Quentin's about the only man I can stand to look at these days. Besides you."

"Thanks."

"He's been wonderful," she said as though by herself.

Hart imagined the walls of the house disappearing, and the grass growing up around them until they couldn't see each other.

"Is he any happier about the baby than you are?" he asked.

"He doesn't know," she said once more into the void before re-entering the space between them.

"Why haven't you told him?"

"It would be easier if he didn't know."

Hart silently asked for further explanation.

"I may not keep it," she said.

"He's going to figure it out eventually," he forced himself to chuckle. "Unless he's spending eight months in Guangdong."

"I'm not talking about adoption."

Hart was thrust backward through time, twenty years, the last moment he had yelled at Megan. He stopped short of yelling, but she could see it in him.

"I'm not sure I want to bring a child into this world. At all."

He was still calming himself down. He almost said, "Then you should have used protection." But that would sound odd at their age.

"Even if I gave it to someone else," Megan kept up her defense, "they would still be out there. He. She. Stuck in a world that values guns more than children."

"Don't use your company's talking points on me."

"Sorry."

"I thought your job was helping. All those laws you've passed."

"I've also learned some things I wish I didn't know."

"Your mother would be devastated."

"She's not going to find out," she glared at him.

Hart felt like they should have been standing up by that point, face to face, arguing their positions. But they were stuck in their seats.

"Unless you keep it," he hoped out loud.

She shrugged and looked away.

Hart stared out the window at all the places he'd rather be.

"Why me?" he asked.

"You deal with things better than Mom or Quentin."

"This is a very different thing. Isn't there someone at work you can talk to? Some hairy-legged woman?"

"I didn't know you were such a pro-lifer."

"It's my grandchild."

"Of course," Megan snapped. "You need a new grandchild. And if this one doesn't make it, I'll pump out another one. I'll keep trying. Again and again until the world is fixed."

She leaned so far back over the couch that she could have looked out the window behind her, seen the world upside down. She covered her face with her hands.

He wanted to comfort her, but didn't think it would go well. He breathed out until he had no choice but to breathe in.

"I've made it," he muttered.

She came out from behind her hands with a scowl and slid into a right-side up position.

"Peak heartlessness," he continued his conversation with himself.

"What are you talking about?"

"Setting goals. Reaching them."

"I don't understand."

"Come to me with your most cold-blooded ideas."

"Dad..."

"Did Quentin put you up to this?"

Megan's jaw plummeted, taking her shoulders with it.

"Well?" he demanded.

"Were you not listening? Did you forget already? Have I rocked your world that much?"

Hart felt like bellowing, ranting, raving about her decisions and what she must think of him, but didn't know how to start, or what to say.

"Yes," he said. "Yes, you have."

It was the aftermath of the shooting all over again. The feeling of being toppled, of time disappearing and the ground beneath him full of earthquakes.

He may have excused himself, he may have just left. Whether he said anything or not, Megan called after him.

"Don't tell anyone!"

He heard her as he reached the door.

"Why would I do that?" he thought, or said out loud. He couldn't discriminate between his thoughts and actions.

He barely made it past the two-lunatic conspiracy paparazzi without getting out of the car and smashing their phones.

He drove toward his house, but missed the turn.

It may have been a mistake at first, for a second.

But he never considered turning around.

His exhaustion from the trip had turned to anxiety. He didn't know what to do with himself, but he had to do something. He thought of veering downtown for beer or coffee. Sitting still didn't sound appealing, though, and neither alcohol nor coffee felt like a good fit.

The thought of coffee had him thinking of the Sons of Liberty and their hangout.

He bypassed downtown and headed back onto the highway, in the opposite direction from where he had been with Peaches earlier that day. He headed back toward the mountains. Their snow-capped peaks captured the setting sunlight. He was able to see them for most of the drive across the flatlands. He didn't know what he was going to do when he reached them, when he climbed back up to the little town where he had declared himself healed. Maybe it would be a reminder. The town could be his touchstone, filled with memories of his daughter and his wife, and of his new love.

But when night had fallen and the mountains were upon him, he admitted there was no going back. He may as well have been boarding a space ship. If he survived this trip, he would find himself in an even stranger land than the one pushing him up the mountain. He saw very little ahead of him: darkness, trees with snow on their branches, and signs telling him to slow down.

Hart pulled into town around the same time he first took his place at the table with the Sons of Liberty, the night before last. He drove slowly past the coffee house and saw them at their usual table. He turned into the parking lot between the coffee house and the dive bar and wondered why he was there. Anger was the easy answer. But he had no idea what he was going to do with his anger.

The drive had put him into a trance. The road was something he could focus on, a fixed point. Unlike the world he passed through, which was so unhinged, so unfit for another grandson. He could hold still, but the vehicle moved forward. Sitting in the lot was not as comforting. The car was as still as he was. He was stuck in that unworthy world, rather than speeding past it.

His car was the only one in the lot. The rest were pickup trucks. He was parked across from them, so he could see them coming, so he wouldn't be surrounded by them. In spite of his restlessness, he stayed inside of his car, turning the ignition every so often to run the heater. He didn't want to be seen with them again. People would assume he was part of their space.

He also wanted to keep his options open.

Some of those options were more drastic than others. All of them could only be carried out if he wasn't identified. He wasn't prepared to surrender. He didn't want to lash out. He wanted to accomplish something. Glenn had shown him what was possible in a world so connected and petulant. He thanked Glenn under his breath.

The coffee house wouldn't close for another hour. He had time to choose.

He put his head back and let his muscles slack, trying to force his brain into relaxation. Then his brain realized that in coming straight up the mountain from Megan's house, he had taken his phone with him. He slumped forward, cursing himself as he crumpled. Whatever he was going to do, it would have to look like an accident.

He pulled out his phone and was surprised to field a signal so high up in the mountains, then deduced he must have been picking up the Wi-Fi signal from the coffee house. Certainly not from the dive bar.

He searched for the Sons of Liberty website. The key words led him through pages of hits filled with historical references before landing on theirs. He recognized the home page, with its eagle in mid-screech and the gothic font meant to arouse the Founding Fathers, but which more loudly evoked a self-published vampire trilogy. The word "membership" caught his eye on the horizontal menu below the eagle's talons. He wanted to address them by name when they came out, but couldn't remember them all, and was hoping the menu item would offer their names, maybe with photos. He laughed at himself when he found none. Of course they didn't want to identify themselves. They had a mission statement, they asked for money, they asked for the reader's contact information, but their names were nowhere to be found.

There were photos in the "news" section, group shots of them protesting at various locations, guns worn and raised. The captions below the shots didn't mention any names, either. They described what they were doing, which was always, more or less, "protecting our freedom." The pictures started to blend together as Hart scrolled through them, turning the images into a single, lengthy shot of angry, yelling faces. Then one leaped out at him and made him reverse course and scroll back up.

They were in front of a school. Hart could see a playground behind a fence in the near distance, and directly behind them was a sign with the name of the school on it and a message board proclaiming that everyone should have a happy Valentine's Day. The caption below the photo read, "You won't see us in the mainstream media getting arrested in front of a school." The next photo down indeed showed them being led away in cuffs, with the caption "If we had gone in the school and shot it up and gotten ourselves killed, we'd be famous. This is what hypocrisy looks like."

Hart closed the site, put down his phone, and thought of ways to grant their wish.

He heard familiar voices, fast-talking and aggressive. One of them cackled like a person who had once been told he had a great laugh. Hart convulsed and woke up.

They were milling around by the beds of their pickups.

There were four of them. He recognized three. Unless one had shaved. It was difficult to tell in the light being cast by the beer signs glowing behind him from the dive bar.

He had fallen asleep before constructing a plan, but they were about to get away. He would have to look for an opportunity and improvise. Maybe it wouldn't happen.

He wanted to find out.

Hart rolled out of his car and hailed them as he approached, using one of the names he remembered.

"Johnny!" he said, turning his nervous energy into something he hoped sounded like enthusiasm.

Johnny was the first one with whom Hart had made eye contact the night before last, so he hoped there would be some kind of simpatico remaining between them. He remembered Wade's name, too, since he was the combative one, but that's also why he didn't want to go with him as the first option.

Johnny squinted at him, along with the others.

The one with the splotchy beard was the first to glow with recognition this time.

"BC!" he raised his arm as though he had won a contest by recognizing him.

He was also the one whose name Hart couldn't remember.

"What's up?" Hart said as he came in for a fist bump.

Having connected with him, he started to use the other names.

"And what's up with you, Johnny?" he said in mock offense. "Tossed me aside already? And you too, Wade?"

"Couldn't see you, man," Johnny got his fist bump. "Thought you were some bar fly from that dump over there."

Wade didn't say anything, but looked friendly enough as they bumped knuckles.

Hart introduced himself as BC to the clean-shaven one, then immediately forgot his name. He was struck by how young he looked. Perhaps it was the lack of beard.

"Aren't you a bit young for coffee?" Hart kidded. "You guys shouldn't get him hooked."

The kid had obviously heard those kinds of jokes before, but the rest laughed at someone else getting in on them.

"Sorry," Hart aimed an apology at him, while the rest were determined to laugh longer and describe to each other what they looked like as they laughed.

"You're all..." Wade said as a lead-in to his imitation of Johnny.

"And you're like..." Johnny fired back with an impersonation of Wade.

While watching the laugh-off, Hart remembered the third one's name.

"And how does Chad laugh?" he asked the group.

The clean-shaven one took advantage of the chance to fire back at someone, and obliged with a biting version of Chad.

"Maybe if you grew a beard this wouldn't happen," Chad sniped.

"Maybe if you grew something else you wouldn't be such a bitch," the kid cracked, which led to another round of braying.

Hart didn't need to pretend to laugh to blend in. A broad smile was enough. As the noise died down, the kid shrugged at Hart as if to finally accept his apology, and assure him he was used to it. Hart appreciated the gesture, but also bristled inside at the idea of bonding with him. He reminded himself to keep them all at a distance.

"What are you doing back here?" Johnny asked.

"I forgot something at the hotel," Hart said. "Told my wife I was coming up after work to fetch it."

"Dumb ass," Wade joked. "What did you forget?"

"Nothing."

Johnny and Chad looked at each other, while Wade and the kid looked at Hart.

"It was an excuse," Hart explained. "Your message stuck with me. I've been thinking about it. About you guys."

"You're not some old fag, are you?" Wade asked.

The other three howled their approval.

Hart took their ragging in stride.

"You guys obviously gave him the wrong idea," the kid turned it back on them. "What are you up to when I'm not around?"

"It's Randy's fault," Johnny clowned. "He was there that night making eyes at poor old BC."

"I remember," Chad played along. "Looked like love to me."

"Love of country," Hart said, which inspired an abrupt end to the jokes, and a solemn moment of silence.

"Sorry, guys," he said on the verge of laughter. "I wasn't patriot-shaming you."

"We deserve it," Johnny said. "I mean, c'mon. We got a new recruit, and we're gonna disrespect the man?"

He slapped Hart on the shoulder.

"That's right," Chad followed up on Johnny's announcement. "Our membership just increased by, like, what?"

"One," Wade smirked.

"I mean by how many percent. That sounds better."

"So eight of us plus one," the kid added.

"Eight?" Wade questioned.

"I know the Bertram brothers never hang out," Johnny answered. "But they come to the demonstrations."

"They came to two," Wade said.

"And we've had eight," Chad offered. "Or, wait. Nine. We've had nine."

"Twelve percent," Hart jumped in, trying to help Chad back up his point about percentages.

But it was Wade who grinned at him.

Hart nodded in return and held the floor.

"So are we gonna stand around the parking lot doing math?" he asked the foursome. "Or are you gonna put me through some sort of initiation?"

The Son of Liberty looked at each other.

"Well..." Chad ventured. "We could get fucked up and shoot cans."

"Right on," Wade agreed.

"My kinda club," Hart said.

"You want a ride, BC?" Johnny asked, gesturing at Hart's car.

"Do I need one?"

"The compound is up the mountain a bit, with a dirt driveway. It's tricky without four-wheel drive."

"I don't want to put you guys out," Hart said. "I need to get back to the hotel later."

"Suit yourself," Johnny said. "We'll hook you up to the winch if you get stuck."

A light snow started to fall as they wound their way up the highway through the pine trees. The driveway was the straightest part of the trip, but as Johnny had warned, it was also the most challenging. For a half mile, Hart felt his car slide three different times. He fell back on his past training to keep his car from drifting into the snowbanks on either side, letting up on the accelerator and steering gently into the slide. His hands held tight to the wheel, while his feet stayed light on the pedals. Chad and the kid were ahead of him, while Johnny and Wade trailed him, each in their own truck. Combined with the canopy of trees overhead and the darkness all around, being stuck in the middle of the convoy was like driving through a tunnel in heavy traffic, despite being miles from civilization. He felt pressure to perform well for them, then chuckled at himself for feeling that way. Nonetheless, when they complimented his driving after they reached the house, he was proud. He parked off to the side, away from their cluster of trucks. The idea was to provide an easier get-away, but it also presented an opportunity for a triumphant approach, as they greeted him with high-fives and fist bumps.

The house was three stories, if one included the basement that was partially dug into the ground beneath the stilted porch that wrapped around the middle floor. They went down a brief flight of cement stairs into the basement, through what could have been the front door, if not for the next story up.

Chad led the way and turned on the lights. The room looked like a hunting lodge that had hosted a frat party. There were gun cabinets filled to capacity, empty beer cans, boxes of ammunition, posters of sweaty, braless women in tank tops, and deer heads mounted on every wall. The furnishing was sparse. A smattering of mismatched chairs that looked as though they had been found on various street corners were backed up against all four walls. The layout suggested they wanted to keep the center clear for any brawls that might break out. There was no table, just a counter in the back that probably served as a bar, since there was a refrigerator behind it that could have held beer, or carrion, or both.

"You guys all live here?" Hart asked.

"This land's been in my family for five generations," Chad said.

"That doesn't answer my question."

The others laughed at Chad, who pretended to laugh back.

"Yeah, we do," Johnny answered for him.

"My folks moved into a condo outside Sacramento a few years back," Chad explained, some disgust in his voice. "Decided it was time to downsize, take it easy."

"So it's ours now," the kid looked on the bright side.

"Unless your sister changes her mind," Wade reminded him.

"Not gonna happen," Chad snapped. "She's better than us now. Remember?"

He reached the refrigerator behind the counter and started pulling out one can of beer at a time, then tossing it to a waiting member.

"How does a woman marry a Mexican, then think she's moved up in the world?" Johnny sneered.

Chad shrugged while he continued his beer toss.

"Must be that college degree," Wade said as he caught his can.

"Like magic," Chad kept one for himself and cracked it open.

The kid opened his, too, but it was still shaken from the toss. The beer foamed over his hand and cascaded to the floor as he jumped back from the landing spot while keeping the can extended as far away from himself as possible.

"I was hoping to prank the new guy," Chad chuckled as the rest of them laughed at the kid.

Hart raised his beer in the kid's direction.

"Thanks for tipping me off," he said.

The kid was too busy sipping from the puddle at the top of his can.

"Think it's safe yet for a toast?" Johnny asked.

"Let's give it a shot," Chad said, coming around the counter to meet them in the middle. "To the new guy!"

"The new guy!" they said, Hart included, and lifted their beers before opening them to the same foamy results as the kid.

They slurped as much as they could from their geysers before surrendering the rest to the floor. Such an enormous first sip reminded Hart that he hadn't eaten since early that afternoon on the drive home with Peaches. The beer was the watery kind he also used to buy when he was their age and looking for the most cans for the least amount of money, but its effects were immediate. He had yet to figure out what he was going to do, and being drunk wasn't going to help. Whatever courage alcohol provided would be undermined by sapped reflexes.

He found a seat in the corner, in a weathered Adirondack chair with a dirty pillow leaning against its back. He was able to hold his beer out of sight, on the far side of the armrest, and pour a little bit out onto the floor after every small sip, which he sucked in with loud swigs to make them sound large. He tried not to talk much, to conserve energy and keep his head clear. He asked them questions before they could ask him any. He asked them why they bring guns to their school demonstrations.

"Just a helpful reminder," Johnny said.

"They're soft targets," Chad chipped in. "Psychos go for the most vulnerable, the places where they can't protect themselves. We want those places to think about that."

"You want them to be armed?" Hart asked.

"Is there a better way to protect yourself?" the kid asked back.

Hart took one of his loud, small sips, then lowered his arm out of sight to pour some more on the floor. Asking questions was leading to discussions that his beer buzz wouldn't allow him to go along with. His belligerence was bubbling up as his inhibitions were flattening. He thought it best to corral them into a situation that involved less talking and more action.

"Didn't you all say something about shooting cans?" he asked.

"Is it still snowing?" Wade wondered aloud.

"Who cares?" the kid answered. "Let's fuckin' squeeze out some rounds!"

There were hoots and hollers. Hart expected them to flock toward one of the gun cabinets, but they each lurched toward a different one, each to their own private collection.

"You got one in the car, BC?" Johnny asked as he opened up his cabinet.

"No."

Johnny stopped what he was doing.

"Well, where is it?"

The others paused to hear the answer.

"Home."

"What the fuck is it doing there?" Wade laughed.

"Home protection," Hart shrugged.

"You have a permit to carry?" Johnny expressed some concern.

"Yes."

"Then why ain't you carrying?" the kid cried.

"What are you guys so afraid of?" Hart asked.

"I ain't afraid of nothing!" the kid carried on as he pulled a pistol from his cabinet and held it across his chest.

"Me, neither," said Chad, likewise brandishing a handgun from his stash. "How 'bout you, Wade?"

"Nope," said Wade, joining the show of force.

"That's what I'm talkin' about," Johnny beamed. "No fear!"

"Scared don't know it!" Chad bellowed.

"Fear don't feel it!" the rest replied in unison.

Hart stood up and approached them. Their revelry faded and they stared at Hart, who stared back. He took a deep breath that dramatized his pause.

"So does this mean I can't borrow a gun?"

They cracked up.

Wade laughed loudest of all.

"Here," he beckoned him over to his collection. "I'm gonna sit this one out, anyway. Not too worried about an empty beer can invasion."

"I'll pay you for the ammo," Hart said.

"No worries," Wade reached into his cabinet and pulled out a nine millimeter for Hart.

"You sure?"

"I like your style," Wade told him as he thrust it into Hart's palm. "You speak your mind. No bullshit."

"Thanks," Hart said, studying Wade to make sure he wasn't actually calling him on all his lies.

The coast looked clear in Wade's eyes.

The snow wasn't falling any harder, but had been falling long enough to leave a thin shroud over all of their vehicles. Hart estimated that if he was going to do something, he'd better do it within the next hour.

When it was his turn to fire, he thought it best to hustle them. If he did anything, it was going to rely on surprise, and keeping his abilities hidden from them would help. The kid had gathered an armful of empty beer cans and placed them on a variety of surfaces, at different sightlines. Some were on a wooden fence, as tradition would seem to dictate, while others were on stumps in a wood pile, and on a rusted tractor, on its seat and its hood.

Hart adopted the misguided stance he had seen so many people start with when his department had offered public lessons at the firing range, a sloppy version of the isosceles: feet too far apart and pelvis thrust forward, as though trying to rub their crotch on the target in addition to shooting it.

"You ever fire a weapon before?" Chad asked.

"Of course."

"Ever fire one properly?" Wade jabbed.

"Nothing wrong with an isosceles," Johnny said.

"If it's done right," the kid scoffed.

"Around here we like the Weaver," Johnny jumped back in. "It's a better fighting stance. And even if we're just shooting cans, we never forget what we're training for."

He stood next to Hart and demonstrated. He turned sideways by sliding back his firing-side leg and explained the benefits of a smaller profile and range of movement. Hart tried his best to do exactly as he said, without instinctively modifying Johnny's tips to suit the subtle preferences Hart had developed over his career.

"Okay," Johnny said upon molding Hart into his idea of the perfect shooter. "Now try."

Hart lined up a can on the hood of the tractor, then deliberately missed by a foot, adding a new hole to the dozens in the side of the machine. Then he added a few more holes into the chassis before missing too high, sending a couple of bullets into the dark forest.

The Sons of Liberty relished the chance to feel superior to someone, laughing and offering more instructions. Hart was starting to have a good time fielding their advice. This would not do. He needed to get back to hating them.

"Maybe if I had a bigger target," Hart said, stepping back from the firing line.

"Nobody here but us white folks," the kid took the bait.

"And whitey too slow," Chad hopped on board. "Not a big help if you're trying to simulate a home invasion."

"Plus we're easier to see in the dark," Johnny joined in.

"Here," the kid stepped forward and took his stance. "Let me show you how to keep the barbarians outside the gate."

He hit every can he aimed for. The others gravitated toward each side of him as they counted out loud. Six in a row. Seven. Eight. The kid paused and punctuated his streak with a yelp.

"God is good!" he added.

"So you guys consider yourselves a Christian organization?" Hart asked.

He was by himself, behind the line they had formed.

The kid turned to glare at him.

"Any group worth belonging to is," he said before turning his attention back to his aluminum enemies.

"Does that surprise you, BC?" Chad asked, barely turning to address him as the kid started firing again.

"A little," Hart shrugged in between shots. "I mean, scaring kids at school, racism...not exactly what Jesus would do."

"The Bible's full of ass-kicking," Wade barked without looking back. "And it makes some pretty clear distinctions between the races. I'm tired of the PC Thought Police trying to turn Jesus into a pussy. He was the most powerful person who ever lived. A goddamn superhero."

"Who never used his power to kill anyone," Hart said. "Even when they were killing him."

"What the fuck, BC?" Johnny spun to face him. "You with us or not?"

Hart smiled.

"I'm keeping you sharp. Every group needs a prick who's willing to ask questions."

Johnny smiled back.

"We've already got Wade," he said, which earned a laugh from Chad and a middle finger from Wade before they all turned their attention back to the kid's display of marksmanship.

Hart remembered the tension between Wade and the others that first night at the coffee house, the deep divide over their goals and their message that anyone in the place could see and hear. He assumed it wasn't a one-night spat. Now he had confirmation.

And he had an idea.

He tucked the gun under his arm and blew into his hands to warm them.

Another shot pierced a can. It spun into the night air and through the falling snow.

Hart drew the gun back out.

"Wade," he called.

Wade turned and Hart stared at the back of the gun as he gestured for Wade to join him, as if he had a question about it. He reluctantly left the kid's side, leaving Chad and Johnny on the kid's other side.

"What's up?" Wade sounded annoyed as he reached Hart's left side.

"Are you right-handed?"

"Yes."

"Good."

"Why?"

"My nine millimeter at home is a little different than this one," Hart said. "I was wondering..."

The kid's last shot rang out.

Hart glanced up and dropped his jaw.

"He missed."

"Really?" Wade looked forward.

Hart pressed the nine to Wade's temple and fired.

Chad and Johnny turned toward the noise behind them out of curiosity more than alarm. They barely had time to register their horror before Hart shot each of them.

The kid saw the bodies fall next to him, and turned with his weapon still raised.

He stared at Hart. His eyes were wide open with confusion, and with something else.

"Are you scared now?" Hart asked him.

The kid pulled the trigger, but was out of ammunition.

Hart was not.

He put him down with one shot, and assessed the scene.

The snow beyond Wade's body was sprayed with a messy streak of fluids and fragments. The other three bodies were more contained. Scattered specks of blood, the rest apparently seeping into the snow beneath them. The snow above them fell harder, or it may have seemed that way because Hart was watching it collect on their bodies. Their blood was already starting to disappear, and their distinguishing features blend into white dust. The cold air kept away any smells. The forest was quiet. No animal or bird noises. Hart could hear the snow landing on the earth. It sounded like someone putting their finger to their lips and saying, "Shhhhh..."

He crouched down next to Wade and wiped Wade's gun with the bottom of Wade's shirt, then used the same section of flannel as a makeshift glove to put the gun in Wade's right hand.

He walked to his car and grabbed the floor mat from the passenger side, then dragged it over the footprints he had left. The snow would cover for him, but he wanted to be certain, if that was possible. He wondered if anyone else would show up. Randy perhaps, or those brothers they had mentioned. It was rather late at night for guests to arrive in most places, but he assumed etiquette didn't apply to the Sons of Liberty compound. He needed to get out and let the snowstorm do its job.

In spite of his concerns about encountering another vehicle headed into the property while he was on his way out, he drove slowly. He could not risk sliding into the snowbanks lining the driveway. Even if he managed to extract himself from one, which was unlikely without help, the process would leave a clue too large for the storm to erase. His hands had yet to thaw, which made gripping the wheel difficult. He held his fingers in front of the heater, one hand at a time, alternating every several seconds. His feeling returned in a rash of stings, as though being delivered through injections rather than by hot air.

Relief at seeing the highway ahead was strangled by a pair of headlights trembling through the trees. They looked as though they'd reach the entrance to the driveway about the same time as Hart. He considered what he might say to someone who passed. He could act panicked and say he was invited to the property and made a grisly discovery. Or he could just pass the other vehicle, give a strategically-placed wave that obscured his face, and hope they didn't remember any details about his car or any part of his license plate.

The lights reached the end of the tunnel that Hart felt he was inside of.

Their brightness passed the entrance to the driveway and proceeded along the highway.

Hart exhaled and his pulse slowed, his adrenalin draining in rhythm with the fading lights.

He encountered only two more vehicles on the way down the mountain into town. One passed by in the opposite direction. The other came up on him from behind. Hart spent a moment imagining one of the Sons of Liberty wasn't dead, had suddenly gasped for air while bolting upright from under a sheet of snow, and staggered to his truck to chase him down. But it was someone with four-wheel drive who thought Hart was driving too slowly, who passed him by on the first straightaway that presented itself.

All the stores and restaurants in town were closed, the hotels run by night managers. Only the signs were lit. Hart was tired but couldn't stop. Checking into a hotel was out of the question. Sleeping in a car by the side of the road or in a parking lot always attracted suspicion. He wasn't familiar enough with the area to know of a discreet place where it was allowed, or at least ignored.

As he passed by a gas station, the most well-lighted spot in town, he noticed blood on his sleeves. He waited until he was outside of town to pull over and change, where the streetlights ended and the highway took people back into the woods and down the mountain, back to where the rest of the world lived. He reached for his travel bag in the backseat and pulled out the clothes he had worn to dinner with Peaches. They smelled of garlic and rosemary, and the lavender body wash Peaches had showered with.

He changed in a hurry.

Before stowing the bloody clothes in his bag, he studied them. There was more than blood. There was fluid that held Wade's thoughts up until an hour ago, that recorded his experiences and turned them into ideas, that now did nothing but stain a shirt.

Everything depends on the right combination. Each thing in isolation is useless. Take something away from its purpose and it dies. Remove a part from a whole and it all collapses. Blood is a liquid. Brain is a solid. Skin is a container.

He woke up with the pile of soiled clothes still on his lap.

Morning light shone gray, the sun yet to rise above the horizon, but on its way.

A truck sped past, disturbing the air around Hart's car enough to make it wobble.

He looked around, convinced there must be a department's worth of officers surrounding his car with their weapons drawn.

The shoulder was empty, the clearing leading into the woods was vacant, and the road hosted an occasional vehicle.

He breathed deeply and wondered if he was lucky or cursed.

Finally finishing the task of stuffing the incriminating clothes in his travel bag, he merged onto the highway.

His heart rate settled by the time he sprang from the other side of the woods, on the downslope of the mountain. But his mind still raced. The dense forest of pine trees gave way to a scattering of oak trees and rocky outcroppings. The sun was now above the trees, its light bouncing off everything in its path. Hart's perspective further lit up the world as he saw it. His vision merged with all his other senses. He was deeply aware of his surroundings. Every tree and its bark, its leaves, and the red-crested woodpeckers hammering away at its trunk. Every rock and its cracks, and the patches of moss clinging to its surface. Every car that passed by and the people inside them, their expressions, the positions they were in the moment Hart captured them.

He had been so involved with time, his relationship to the past, his role in the future. His physical presence depended on it. On this drive home, however, on this escape from death, he felt beyond physical, a life force unattached to a timeline.

When he reached the base of the mountain, though, and found himself advancing closer to civilization, his point of view couldn't keep up with the mounting assortment of human inventions. The traffic lights, the fences, the doorways, the words on the street signs and on the billboards and on the storefronts, all of it formed a cluster that was palpable but forgettable. Guilt faded as the stimuli collected.

He thought of the kid's face when the kid realized he had no ammunition.

"It's too bad what happened to that kid," Hart said to himself. "But..."

He said it all the way home. Sometimes aloud, sometimes in his head, in a variety of tones, always with the same ending:

But.

CHAPTER 7

Hart felt less remorse than he had in the aftermath of Glenn. He hoped this sneaking sense of acceptance didn't represent a trend, and was more troubled by that possibility than by what he had actually done.

In addition, when the narrative surrounding the Sons of Liberty shooting conformed to his imagination of it, with Wade portrayed as a disgruntled member who perpetrated a murder-suicide, Hart felt an embarrassing twinge of resentment. He didn't want credit, but he wanted people to understand that someone had pulled off a remarkable feat. He wanted people to be impressed by him, while not knowing who he was.

His daughter's cause was helped by his fabrication, which helped him rationalize his actions to even greater self-satisfaction. Many an article picked up on the notion that most gun deaths are the product of domestic disputes rather than mass shootings, and perhaps the Sons of Liberty dispute was large and fratricidal enough to draw attention to the threat that households posed to themselves. Such was the case being made on one side, at least. On the other side, however, was the story of a militia lacking discipline, not characteristic of the restraint and camaraderie exercised by the vast majority of hate groups, as Hart liked to interpret their argument.

Even deeper on that side was a narrative involving a set up. For once, Hart mused, they were right. It was staged. Run with that thought, he encouraged them from afar. But of course when it came to who was responsible, they were wrong. They went with their old standby, the government. He could see their point, Hart flattered himself. Who else could possibly pull that off? Maybe another group who was stooging for the feds, some hypothesized. Or maybe Wade was a mole for the feds, and the ongoing deception of his friends drove him to suicidal rage. Not that they ever said "maybe". Each author of a given conspiracy was quite positive they were right. And to prove it, they had some links to other people's websites who agreed with them. But the feds were always involved somehow. Every story ended up there. All of these theorists claimed to have faith in the people, yet refused to believe a private citizen was capable of what Hart had done.

Perhaps, he imagined, they could begrudgingly admire him if they ever found out, even though it involved killing their teammates.

But the team is all that mattered. Their world was a handful of true believers, and all those others who just didn't get it. And he was sewing unease in their clubhouse. It wasn't an intruder who would get you, nor an awkward co-worker or classmate. It was your friends and family. Which was the whole point of the Sons of Liberty Massacre, as it was being dubbed.

No. There was no way they could admire him.

"I can't believe we were just there," Peaches said as she looked at her phone and dragged her finger along the screen.

"Where?" Hart half-laughed.

The half that wasn't laughing was composed of mild irritation. They may have been in the early stages of their relationship, but he had picked up on her habit of making vague statements heavy on pronouns and prepositions, but light on details, that he was supposed to understand all the same.

"You know where," she said.

And he did in this case, but just as easily could not have known, which was often the case.

"That Italian restaurant off the park?" he held fast to playing dumb.

She lowered her phone and tilted her head.

"What would possibly have happened there?"

"Health code violations?"

"That massacre."

"There was a massacre at the Italian restaurant?"

She went from a stare to a glare.

"Are you kidding?" her words added ice.

"Of course," he stated the obvious.

"After what happened to this community? At that school?"

She didn't even live in this community when it happened, he thought, and almost reminded her of this fact as his look plummeted to an even lower temperature than the one she gave him.

But he would be lashing out. This was not the way he wanted to tell her about Stanley.

"You're right," he used his words like a calming deep breath.

"Is something the matter?" she asked.

"Just a little embarrassed."

He embraced the tension. It provided even better camouflage than humor when it came to keeping himself from revealing any role in the massacre she was reading about.

No one was ever as good at feigning innocence as they thought they were. It was safest to assume he was as bad at it as the criminals he had encountered in his life. His humility and realism were confined to that assumption, however, as he refused to think of himself as a criminal. Which made him all the more like one.

He didn't have victims, he had targets.

He wasn't taking revenge, he was motivating change.

He was not guilty.

They were never guilty.

Maybe a few admitted guilt, but he had forgotten them. It was easy to forget the reasonable, and remember the preposterous. We have stories to tell, and we want them to be interesting.

"Maybe some good can come of this," Peaches said.

Hart gathered she was apologizing for calling him out so aggressively on his callous joke, without actually saying she was sorry.

"I suppose," he accepted her treaty. "But I'm not sure what that good would look like."

He had an idea about that, too, but wanted confirmation.

"If something like this happens among gun lovers," she said, "instead of at a school or a movie theatre, then maybe they'll start to pay attention."

He wanted to raise a fist and let out a whoop.

"Is that what some people are saying?" he asked instead.

He knew they were. He had scanned the editorials and blogosphere, and had waded into the sludge of the comment threads. But he wondered how big a number they represented.

If he wanted to maintain the momentum he seemed to be creating, he couldn't rely on things breaking his way as consistently as they had so far.

For one, he couldn't plan on running into his next target in person. That would not only take too long, if it happened at all, but would also localize his spree, tightening the radius of where the incidents had taken place, these incidents that were demonstrating a pattern. He would have to find his possibilities online, and travel to follow through on them.

He didn't use any of his own electronics to conduct his search. He used the library, or the computer store downtown, or the electronics section at one of the box stores, while wearing a hat and reading glasses. He fished the stream of comments that ran beneath the articles covering what he had done. He sought the most belligerent, aggressive posters. Hart found those types usually left their profiles wide open, perhaps to prove how unafraid and unrepentant they were. He would click on their names, and find them posing with their guns in their profile pictures, spouting expletives and daring anyone to tell them what to do, or even question them.

There were dozens of promising candidates. He started to whittle them down by state, focusing on those with the most lenient gun laws. He wanted to maintain his practice of using their own weapons against them, and thought a private sale gone wrong would be an effective set-up. That was the initial read on the Glenn scene, after all.

Hart found several posters who were charged up over a massive gun show about to take place a couple of states away. Some of them were planning on trolling the floor for buyers who wanted a quicker sale than the licensed dealers could offer. It was a drivable distance that would still put some space between his latest act and his next.

He told Nando he was taking another roadie with Peaches.

He told Peaches he was going to a retired cop benefit with Nando.

Megan and Quentin were both out of town.

He used a website dedicated to buying and selling between the locals of the host city to book the most discrete room possible, a detached studio in a backyard belonging to someone who said he could leave cash on his way out.

He was able to make the drive in one day, early morning to late night. He parked down the street from the house with the studio and left before the sun came up. He made a joke to himself about a one-night stand as he thumbed through the small stack of twenty-dollar bills one last time before dropping it on the dresser. He turned up the collar of his jacket against the morning chill, and to shield his profile in case someone in the house was up early, looking out the window.

The convention center was in a sprawling suburban outpost with a parking lot larger than the venue itself. Hart wasn't worried about using the cover of night this time. He parked in the outskirts of the lot, and while inside the center, gravitated toward sections of the floor that were farther away from the cameras. He would ask any side dealer who approached him what he was selling, and where he was parked.

The third man who solicited him had both the gun and the parking spot that Hart was looking for. The man wasn't quite elderly, and appeared to be trying to stave off old age by working on his arms quite a bit, but at the expense of any other forms of exercise. He wore a tight t-shirt to show off his arms, and perhaps to gird his belly. Hart gave the man a five-minute head start, then exited through a different door to catch up with him.

The man waved him over to his car. There were two people between Hart and his target. He avoided them by walking one aisle down from them, while shading his eyes and looking away as he passed.

The man had his trunk open. The weapon he had promoted to Hart was the only one on display, a .22 caliber semi-automatic handgun.

"Light inventory," Hart commented.

"Sold two others yesterday," he said.

"Same gun?"

The man nodded as he reached in and handed it to Hart for inspection.

"Men like to buy them for their wives and girlfriends," he explained. "That what you're doing?"

"What if I'm not?" Hart grinned as he turned away from the man to aim it at the distance.

The man chuckled.

"No judgments. I respect my customers."

Hart remained facing away from the dealer. He put the gun in his jacket pocket, then pulled it out as though drawing it on an attacker.

"Is that why you don't run them through a background check?"

"I respect their rights."

"But not the law."

"What's the point?" he said. "Murder's against the law. It still happens."

Hart put the gun in his jacket pocket again and felt for the magazine full of ammunition he had left there.

"So many laws..." Hart reflected out loud.

"Too many," the man liked where this was headed.

Hart held onto the bottom of his jacket as though trying to line up the zipper, using the action to hold the gun steady as he slid the magazine into it.

"Why not just let everyone carry?" Hart said as the gun clicked to life.

"Why not?" the man agreed.

Hart followed through on zipping up his jacket, then pulled the weapon. He held it aloft in front of him, slowly surveying the lot for anyone else passing by.

He saw no one.

He lowered the gun and turned to face the dealer, looking past him to see if anyone was on the other side.

There was nobody innocent behind him.

Hart trained the gun on him.

He went for a chest shot to make sure he hit him.

Two of them, to make sure he killed him.

He didn't catch the look on the man's face any more than he had caught his name.

He took out the magazine and put it back in his jacket pocket. He took out a trim packet of disinfectant wipes from his back pocket and cleaned off the gun. The tight shirt was doing a fine job of keeping the blood close to the wound, while the smell of excrement and urine kept the scene from being too sanitized.

There was no need to make it look like anything other than what it was, a dealer selling to the wrong person. A crafty and careful version of the wrong person, and one clearly trying to make a point. He left the gun on the dealer's chest, just above the wound. People would know this was someone with a plan. Hart would get the credit he was ashamed to find himself wanting at times.

He sensed it wouldn't be so much about his ingenuity, however, and more about the carelessness of the dealer. He could already visualize the comments that would fly from the keyboards of the fetishists, the ones who knew better, who would have conducted a foolproof sale, or, of course, would have shot him before he shot them. They were always quick on the draw, action heroes who were undefeated in the imaginary battles they fought. They would spit on the memory of a man they never met to keep that self-styled winning streak alive, a man who had been on their team.

Perhaps it was more like family than a team, Hart thought as he drove across the desert in the middle of the afternoon. Or like ethnicity. Fellow gunners can make fun of their own, but everyone else had better back off.

The mountains rising above the desert floor had traces of wildflowers sprouting from the late winter rains. Or was it early spring?

Most of the patches were yellow, with occasional splashes of orange, and even smaller speckles of purple, which were harder to see. Hart tried to put aside his projections on what the response to his latest target would be, and instead take stock of his emotions. He checked himself for remorse, running through the possibility that the man had children and grandchildren. They merely led him back to Stanley, and how the man most likely felt about Stanley's death, given that he was selling firearms to strangers at a gun show.

So not only was this target his most clinical, it also inspired the least regret. The x-axis and y-axis were headed for a crossroads. Efficiency was trending upward, emotion downward.

Emotion, that is, as it applied to his targets.

He felt no less connected to those closest to him.

"I have something to tell you," he announced to Peaches.

He had arrived home late the previous night and had to wait all day until she was done with her shift at the hospital. By the time he was able to race to her doorstep, he couldn't be bothered with saying hello.

"Clearly you do," she said, rearing back slightly.

"You asked me if I had grandchildren, and I said no."

"Why would you lie about that?"

"Technically it's true. Now. It didn't used to be."

He started to cry. He had rehearsed what he was going to say all day, in his head, but had yet to say anything out loud. He tried to make sense of why it was happening while it was happening. It had been that long, apparently, since he had talked about Stanley in such a forthright manner. Stanley had merely been alluded to, or simply understood to have been there, hovering over conversations that referenced him but didn't need to explain him.

Now here he was again, and there he went, and Hart wanted nothing more than to hold him once more, even for a second. He would give everything he had, his own life, for that moment, with no regard for what might happen afterwards, no concern for whether he had to answer for anything.

Peaches held him.

He managed to tell her how it happened.

She remembered the remark she had made about the shooting, apologized for it, and fretted over whether she had used it at any other point in any offending manner.

"You didn't know," he assured her. "I could have stopped you."

"You needed to tell me on your own terms," she assured him back.

They embraced in her door frame, agreeing silently to do so for as long as they needed to.

"I do things to forget him," he whispered in her ear. "I don't want you to be one of those things. I want this to be real."

She leaned back and thanked him. She may have said the words, she may have merely looked at him. They went back in for another hug.

"Instead of forgetting him," she ventured to say, "you should do things to make the world better in his name."

His body started to shake.

She said she was sorry.

Hart assumed she was apologizing for making him cry again.

But he was laughing.

He tried to think of an excuse for why, in case she caught on. He never did, but she never noticed, as the effort he made to come up with a reason doused the emotion.

CHAPTER 8

It wasn't just the gun apologists who were speculating that someone was hunting their kind. It was on everyone's mind who followed such events. The general public didn't pay as much attention to the gun dealer murder as they did to the Sons of Liberty story, or Glenn. Not as many imaginations were captured. But those who were plugged into the daily flow of the debate found the scene in the parking lot fascinating, a flash point that brought together all of the opposing perspectives to share their hypotheses. They all agreed that someone was trying to make a point. The question was whom, or what.

The usual accused the government, but within that camp there was some disagreement over whether it was a conspiracy or a rogue agent, or maybe a group of rogue agents. Some wondered at what point an agent can even be considered part of the government anymore.

The other side appeared to coalesce around the idea that a faction was developing in the gun community, that the more moderate forces were pushing back against the more extreme, and trying to show them the consequences of ceding law and order to the gun. Hart appreciated one commenter who wrote, "Jungle law is bad enough without guns in the jungle."

It made him feel like Tarzan, more myth than man.

Reading up on the legend of himself also forced him to face a daunting truth about his future as a lobbyist.

If he wanted to keep focus on his message rather than himself, he would have to be progressively more inventive and alter his tactics. If he simply authored a string of targets, he would be nothing more than a shooter with a signature, a profile, rather than a message. The message would be buried under the bodies. No one would listen to somebody so obviously psychotic. It had to look like a movement, not a lone gunman.

He let that mission statement guide his next move, which was actually two moves.

The first one was the target. He compiled an all-star team of bellicose commenters from the threads that extended from the bottom of the articles regarding the gun dealer incident. He followed the rantings of his team members for a week, looking for clues as to where they spent their time, in addition to gauging their hate levels. A most valuable player started to separate himself from the pack. His posts were no more repugnant and callous than his competitors, but Hart was drawn to the way he signed off every tirade with "COME AND GET IT" and a middle-finger emoji.

He decided to oblige him.

His profile held some photos of him at a makeshift gun range. He wrote captions that fantasized about seeing the faces of his enemies in the tree trunks and pieces of paper he shot. His enemies were anyone who disagreed with him. His imaginary battlefield was located near a state park in his home county, according to the location tag attached to the captions. And according to the time stamps, he liked to go there on a distinct rotation of days and times. Hart needed two days to drive there. He slept in his car on the way and paid cash for gas.

The second move involved another parking lot gun transaction. Upon arrival, he used a computer in the town library to find a couple of locals looking to make a sale. He set up a new email account and used it to correspond with them. The first to respond won his business. He printed a copy of the winning ad and took it with him.

He met the winner at a rest stop on the way to the state park. There was a smattering of travelers stretching and using the restroom. He arrived early and parked in the spot farthest away from where he stood pacing, impersonating a rookie criminal so his dealer would be able to identify him, but not his car. When the dealer arrived, the exchange took less than a minute. The gun was the man's most distinguishing feature.

Hart had to be more patient in waiting for his target to appear. He dozed in his car on the edge of the wilderness with the window open. He could hear gunfire in the distance, throbbing through the trees.

As the latest outburst of echoes flapped through the air, Hart kept his eyes on the sky, imagining the sound waves were visible. He would be able to trace the source, see where the ripples started from, gun shots being the rock dropped in the water. The shooting was happening nearby, and there were no other roads exiting the area. This must be the place, he kept telling himself. The target would reveal himself eventually. What would his voice sound like? Would he be shorter or taller than he projected? What if he came across as a nice guy in person? How accurate a reflection of him was his online personae?

Hart noticed the shooting had stopped and wondered for how long. A little less time than his head had been in the clouds. He heard engines that snarled loud enough to prove how much they had been modified. Two raised pickups came growling to a stop where the forest parted for the road. The trucks looked similar, as did the drivers, but Hart thought one looked a little more familiar. They pulled up next to each other to exchange a few words, and as they pulled away into opposite turns, one extended his arm out the window and flipped his buddy a middle finger.

"That's my man," Hart said aloud as he started his engine.

He tailed him into the nearest town, a hit-and-miss collection of businesses five stoplights long. His target turned at the last lighted intersection into a residential neighborhood. Hart sighed. His man was heading home instead of hanging out. He couldn't bear another stakeout. His back was tightening up and ready to spasm. He decided to head to his target's favorite bar and wait to see if he showed up later.

The owner called it a "bar and grill", which was a generous use of the term, but Hart found his burger to be quite tasty. Maybe because he hadn't eaten much the past two days, but it was enjoyable nonetheless, and when his man entered before he was down to his last bite, his luck appeared to be aligning. His target was even wearing a dark t-shirt with the white likeness of an AR-15 on it, the stars and stripes in mid-billow behind it, as if to confirm his identity. Hart finished his burger and nursed his beer as he watched more members of the crew come in. His target liked to be the center of attention. He had a laugh that sounded more like a sidekick than a villain, and he loved to show it off, often in conjunction with his own jokes.

Hart ordered another beer when the barmaid finally pulled herself away from the attention being lavished on her by the target group. He realized halfway through his second round that it was going to be a lengthy night. His man showed no signs of giving up the spotlight before closing time. He had already found a half-dozen ways to express the importance of following through when pulling a gun.

"If anyone is left to talk about it, you're fucked," went one of his recitals. "So if you pull, you'd better make sure your version of the story is the only version."

Hart closed out his check and headed back to his car to stay sharp while he waited him out. He positioned his car between his man's truck and the door to the bar, then set the alarm on his watch to last call before settling in for a nap.

When the tone sounded, he stepped out of the driver's seat to limber up before the target and his audience poured out. He knew his man would be the last one to head for his truck, since he enjoyed holding court so much. Hart climbed back into his car as they spilled through the door as a group, and sure enough, his target had the last word with each as they peeled away from the crowd one-by-one.

Hart put on a pair of surgical gloves, and took his new gun out from under the seat. When his target was down to his last drinking buddy, that conversation lasted the longest of the good-byes. Hart wiped the prints one more time and briefly considered taking them both out, but he had nothing against the new guy other than his own impatience.

After several sighs from Hart and as many eye rolls, his target broke free. His man was finally alone, giving his signature middle finger to his buddy who drove away.

Hart opened his window as the target approached.

"You sure have a lot to say," Hart lobbed his way.

The target stopped.

"What?" he glared.

"There's an expression about how wise people keep their mouths shut and stupid people won't stop opening theirs, but I can't remember it exactly."

"Do I know you?" the target squinted.

Hart watched the final buddy's taillights disappear. He supposed it wouldn't take long for the bartender and barmaid to clean up and close down.

"Would it make a difference?" Hart asked.

"Whaddya mean?"

Hart opened the door and rose from inside the car, holding the gun low and standing at an angle to keep it hidden.

"If you knew someone personally who disagreed with you, would you still want to kill them?"

"What the fuck are you talking about?"

"You don't like spending time with people who challenge you."

"Look, man..."

"None of the yes-men in there seem willing. Then again, how could they get a word in? You never shut up."

"Fuck you."

"Humor me," Hart said, then revealed the gun by casually pointing it at him. "I'm curious."

The target froze.

"C'mon," Hart beckoned him with the gun. "We don't have much time. We'll have a couple of witnesses out here in a moment, and I know how you feel about witnesses."

"Man, I don't know what your deal is…"

"Does it matter? I'm threatening you. You can pull on me. Let's do this."

"I'm not carrying."

"What?" Hart nearly laughed. "I thought laws were for pussies. I'm quoting you."

"Barry doesn't like us bringing guns into his bar."

"And you agree?"

"He's a private citizen."

"Rules are good. Laws are bad."

"I guess. Yeah."

"Then you'd better get your gun, because I disagree."

The target tried to understand.

"I'm playing by your rules," Hart reminded him. "And playing very fairly. I assume you have a weapon in the truck."

"It's got a lock on it."

"I'll wait."

The target walked to his truck. Hart followed.

He reached inside the glove box and pulled out the gun, then reached inside his pants pocket for his keychain. It shook in his hand as he found the right key. He had even more difficulty putting it into the lock.

Hart glanced at the door to the bar.

"Let's keep Barry and his girl out of this," he said.

"I'm trying," the target barked.

"Here," Hart gestured for the gun and key with one hand while holstering his own gun into the back waistband of his pants with the other.

The target handed over the gun. Hart unlocked it, and was perturbed at how little his own hands shook. He considered letting the loudmouth win, but not for long. If he was going to turn a mission into a suicide, he wanted it to be with someone he respected, someone he would be honored to be shot by.

"This isn't going to look good on you," Hart said as he handed the gun and lock back to his target while re-drawing his own. "They'll find powder from my gloves on your gun and the lock, and know that I did this for you before I shot you."

"Unless I shoot you first."

Hart shot him.

"I'm not a piece of paper stuck to a tree," he told him as the target cursed and struggled for breath.

He took out the copy of the online ad for the murder weapon that he printed out at the library, and wrapped the merchandise in the paper. He was going to leave it on the target's chest, as he had with the man at the gun show, but this one had another minute of life in him, and Hart couldn't afford to wait. The bullet had pierced the symbol of the AR-15 on his shirt. Blood surged up through the hole and drenched the stars and stripes that surrounded it.

He left the package on the pavement next to his target, and drove off.

He was on the highway a mile outside of town by the time an ambulance sped past in the opposite direction on its futile charge.

On the surface, the aftermath of his latest trick looked a lot like his post-Glenn depression. But this time was pure exhaustion, having driven almost all day for four days straight. In calculating his travel plans, he had been more focused on getting there, and a two-day drive didn't seem so daunting. It was the round trip that caught up with him. He stayed in bed, either sleeping or catching up with texts and emails on his phone. He told everyone he was under the weather, which wasn't entirely false.

Nando stopped by in the mornings to check on him, and Peaches stopped by in the evenings.

Megan stopped by, but only after he was feeling better.

She had Quentin in tow. He was standing next to her with a hint of petulance, a child that was forced to come along.

She opened with, "I know you like to be left alone when you're not feeling well."

"I do?" Hart took stock of their past as best he could in a second.

"That's always the impression I got."

"Okay, then. Thanks for waiting. Hello, Quentin."

Quentin waved.

"Nice to see the two of you together."

"It is," he realized.

"You look less than happy. On your way to do some shopping?"

"No," Megan answered. "We came to talk to you."

"Well that it explains it, then."

"Sorry..." Megan tried to follow up on her apology with an excuse.

"Relax," Hart assured her. "There's obviously something on your mind and I'm messing up your script. Come on in and get back on track."

He led them into the house.

"Where to?" he asked. "Out on the patio?"

"No," Quentin answered a little too emphatically.

"Kind of chilly this morning," Hart noted the tone in his voice. "Would you be okay with the kitchen if I close the blinds?"

"Dad..." Megan laughed a little too loudly.

"Or maybe we should go into the laundry room and turn on the dryer."

He turned to face them. Everyone suddenly seemed twenty-five years younger.

"Let's just go with the living room," Megan said.

They each sat separately. Hart took the couch, while Megan and Quentin chose the chairs on each side of the coffee table.

Hart acknowledged everyone's position.

"Talk to me or interrogate me?"

Megan and Quentin looked at each other. She appeared to grow stronger and Quentin shrink as their staring contest played on. Megan reached a point where she gained the power to speak.

"Quentin wants to apologize for approaching you with that idea."

Hart considered how best to react.

"No need," he decided. "Like I told him then, I understand."

"I'm right here," Quentin raised his hand.

Hart chuckled.

"Emotions are more powerful than reason," he assured them.

They each nodded in their own way, Megan more vigorous, Quentin more plaintive.

Hart looked back and forth at them, slowly, as though watching a badminton match between two people who keep missing the birdie.

Megan's nod was the first to fade.

"Funny thing is," she said. "When Quentin told me about coming to see you, I thought of the militia up in the mountains. And I was all, 'no way.'"

"It was a murder-suicide," Hart reminded her.

"I know, I know. But I traced the timeline, and you were up there after Quentin talked to you."

"I came home the day before it happened. That day we talked."

He fixed her with a look to remind her of the secret they shared about her baby.

Megan was undaunted.

"It seemed like the kind of thing someone would do if they knew what they were doing."

"What about the other incidents," Hart pried. "Those private sale murders."

"You've heard of them?" Megan acted surprised. Acted a little too much.

"What private sale murders?" Quentin asked.

"They're half a dozen states away from here and from each other," Megan explained. "They're pretty much local news stories. Only gun news junkies would know about them."

"Which of course I am."

"Of course," Megan conceded.

"They definitely fit the kind of pattern Q's plan was supposed to show off."

Hart wondered why he was pushing it. He had let a chance to excuse himself and invite them to lunch pass by.

"Indeed," Megan agreed.

Father and daughter looked at each other for a lengthy few seconds.

"They certainly do," she finally added.

"So what happened with these private gun sales?" Quentin asked.

"Would you like to explain, Dad? Or should I?"

"Go ahead," he gestured.

He figured it was best to let her describe the events. He might include something that wasn't contained in the news accounts. She gave Quentin a cursory version of each.

"Wow," he said. "That's eerie. Like Hart said, it's the kind of thing we were hoping for."

The way Quentin delivered his line struck Hart as just that: a line reading. He wondered how choreographed their visit was.

"And is it accomplishing what you hoped it would?" Hart asked Megan.

She sighed.

"Not really," she said. "Not yet."

"Is your firm spreading the word?"

"We are. But you know how that goes. People read our work because they agree with us. They don't need convincing. And if you're following the stories, you already know what the gun lover position is."

"A couple of yahoos who don't represent the vast majority of responsible gun owners."

"See how easy their job is?" Megan smirked.

"And the perpetrators are random wackos. Old hippies with guns."

"The guy they got a description of doesn't look like an old hippie, though."

"There's a picture of him?" Quentin asked.

"Police sketch," Megan clarified. "We think we might be able to do something with it. He looks like every middle-aged white guy in America."

"Middle-aged?" Quentin followed up.

Hart nearly rolled his eyes. Flattery?

Megan picked up on Quentin's cue.

"The dealer who sold him the gun described him as older, but a lot of the chatter is convinced it must be the work of a younger man. I split the difference."

She grinned at her father before continuing.

"If he strikes again, we can push his profile harder. Emphasize he's one of them. Create suspicion around their friends and neighbors. Panic at the gun range."

"Which would just be another call to arms," Hart halted her momentum. "That's what I told Quentin when he ran it by me. That's why it won't work."

"This guy seems to think it will," Quentin said.

"If it really is one person," Megan said.

Hart was tempted to tear down the curtain.

"Just ask," he wanted to say. Ask him if he authored any of the stories they were tapping around like a balloon they were trying to keep from hitting the floor.

But he wanted to protect them. If the conversation became direct, he would have to lie, and being evasive was much easier. When the day came that they were questioned, he wanted them to be able to say in all sincerity that they suspected him, but couldn't bring themselves to ask. So rather than throw off the veil, he tightened and adjusted it.

"If you were them, or him," he addressed both Quentin and Megan, but assumed his daughter would take the lead. "And you really wanted to accomplish something, make your mark in the great debate, what would you do?"

Megan and Quentin gaped at one another and appeared to compile their cases for the argument they would have later on concerning who blew their cover.

"Hypothetically speaking, of course," Hart interrupted their silent deliberations.

As he expected, Megan was able to compose herself first and field the question.

"My heart would want to light up every bonkers shithead who paces around in front of our driveway with a camera phone and a conspiracy theory. Head shots, every one of them. Right between the eyes."

This was clearly a recurring fantasy.

"But that would be stupid," she said. "That would bring suspicion to our doorstep. And we want to keep the action as far away from us as possible."

"True," he said flatly, as though filling in a blank space on a quiz.

"Besides, it would fit the pattern that's plaguing the operation."

"Oh?"

"The people he's been going after are clichés," she continued. "And they have no power."

Hart may have taken her by surprise with his bluntness, but she had clearly thought a lot about how she would like to use this secret weapon.

"I see his point," she acknowledged. "Show them it's all in the family. Turn their weapons against them. But they've been through all that. Parking lot arguments, suicides. They don't even count suicides as gun deaths in their world. They claim it's no different than jumping in front of a train or hanging from a beam in the garage. And they know selling guns out of a trunk can go wrong. They know young men high on testosterone can turn on each other in the course of a temper tantrum. That's the cost of doing business. That's life. And even if any of the people directly affected by these stunts change their tune, what can we do with them? Have their children hold up pictures of them? What would the signs say? 'My Daddy Didn't Deserve to Die in a Gun Show Side Deal.' 'Keep Guns Out of Barroom Brawls.' Who cares? They're not sympathetic. That's one thing me and the gun nuts agree on. Those people were stupid assholes."

Hart felt chastised.

Quentin laughed a little, and Hart piggybacked on his laugher with some of his own.

"If this person, these people, want to get something done," Megan pressed on. "They need to go after people who have some clout."

"Those people with clout can't spread the word if they're dead," Hart said.

"You don't kill them," she shot back. "You kill what's dear to them."

It was easy for Hart not to betray any emotion. Her words immobilized him.

"It's nothing new," she acknowledged, relegating death to the context of her plan. "People holding up pictures of their loved ones. On the surface, same old, same old. Only this time it wouldn't be liberal parents from some affluent school district. It would be the very people who used to block those parents from doing anything about it."

Hart needed some time to thaw out.

"That's barbaric," he said at last, barely clinging to the pretense they still indulged.

Megan shrugged.

"I'm a very passionate activist."

He needed time to process what his daughter was suggesting. Quentin didn't appear at all fazed. He had heard it before.

Hart couldn't take that time in their presence. Lunch was out of the question. He invented a date with Peaches that he claimed he needed to get ready for. Not that Megan and Quentin needed any prodding. They appeared to have agreed that their overture to go after the loved ones of the armed and powerful would be their cue to exit, that there wouldn't be anything left to say once it filled the air.

He managed to give Megan a hug, and a slight wave to Quentin, who apologized one more time.

"Sorry to put you through that," he said.

Hart brushed him off.

"It's been too long since I've had the two of you over," he assured him.

"I mean my original pitch," Quentin clarified. "From several weeks ago."

"Oh," Hart had forgotten why they had first claimed to be there. "Right."

"Guess we got a bit off track," Quentin forced a laugh.

Megan forced a smile.

They showed themselves out.

Hart stood in place after the door closed. He spun his daughter's strategy in as flattering a manner as possible. Perhaps it was merely to test her father. If he did it, then they would turn him in.

His phone pinged from the kitchen, announcing a text.

Maybe Peaches got off early. Maybe he really could have lunch with her.

It was from Megan.

"Thanks for not telling Q about the pregnancy."

He noticed she couldn't bring herself to use the word "baby". But then he didn't feel much like talking about it, either.

"So you're letting Q drive?" he texted back.

She didn't respond. He sent another one.

"You're welcome."

She responded to that.

"I love that I can trust you," she wrote.

He didn't know what to say. He didn't feel worthy of the compliment.

If he didn't say anything, she would text some more. They might start arguing about the baby. Then she would drop off Quentin, come back, and argue with him in person.

He looked for an emoji.

He couldn't decide between the cartoon hand giving the okay sign, and the one giving the thumb-up sign, so he went with both.

CHAPTER 9

He kept waiting for nightmares to come.

He rarely remembered his dreams. Hart always thought that was because his career, and his life for that matter, had been smooth up until retirement. It was an icy kind of smooth, rather than warm and soft, but smooth nevertheless. Even when he would wake up with a dream or two on his mind from the previous night's sleep, they were forgettable. He would encounter something horrific on the job, the survivor of an accident screaming for help from the wreckage, and expect to toss and turn and wake up sweating over it. But at most he would dream of going to work without his shoes on, and embarking on a frustrated search for them.

He assumed that would change once he started his work to honor Stanley. The faces of his targets would stalk his dreams. Their voices would whisper in his ear and he would lurch upright in bed screaming.

But his dreams remained too mundane to stick with him. The only one related to his mission happened after his cloaked conversation with Megan and Quentin. And it didn't even happen overnight. It snuck up on him during a nap he took after they left.

In the dream, he watches his video, his six seconds of Stanley.

Only it's not on his phone. It's on a big flat screen television mounted on a wall in the living room, far bigger than the one he actually has.

And the video isn't Stanley. It's Megan when she was Stanley's age.

And it's not on video. She's standing there in front of him.

And she's not Stanley's age anymore.

"How can I be sure it's you?" he asks her.

She holds up a recycling bin filled with clothes she wore as a little girl. Her Velcro tennis shoes with sparkly light blue stars streaking across the side, the pink sleeveless shirt with a floppy collar shaped like a flower petal, the yellow sweatshirt with a brown felt giraffe extending his neck up one side, eating an ice cream cone seven-scoops high extending up the other side.

"How could you forget?" she asks back.

She dumps the clothes on the floor. They don't form a pile. Each item has its own place. Hart looks at them and notices certain details: the pink ponies, the rainbows, the cartoon animals, the words "friends", "sharing", and "love". His mood sinks from confusion to sadness before he wakes up.

He reacquaints himself with the physical world, and wonders if something really happened after no one is left to remember it.

He couldn't carry out Megan's plan. Families were out of the question.

But he wanted to help. He thought he understood her pain. Instead he underestimated it. Why else would she suggest something so monstrous?

He deliberated over ways he could satisfy her goals without following her directions. He focused on the powerful, and considered other things that may be "dear to them."

There was the desire to maintain power. To feel above the rest. To keep that control, or at least the illusion of it, within their group. He had joked with Megan about the Powerful Dead not having a voice, but that assumed none were left standing. If a select few were targeted, there would be plenty left over to change the story holding up their platform.

He wouldn't go after loved ones. Respected ones would have to do.

He could keep it local. If it was a test being proctored by Megan and Quentin, he may as well take it at the most convenient location. Besides, he had spent the last couple of cases in other time zones, and this was a very different target than his last local hit.

The person who punched Glenn to death in a parking lot would not fit the profile of the person who took out a state assemblyman.

The assemblyman he had in mind was such a staunch gun advocate that Hart wondered if he had a stance on any other issue. A visit to his website proved that he did, but attending one of his rallies showed his heart belonged to guns.

A campaign rally wasn't really necessary. It was not a competitive district. But if it made him look busy, and made him money, Hart could hardly blame him.

His office was in the county seat, of course, but his home was at the opposite end of the county from where Hart lived. The distance was comforting as far as leaving a trail was concerned, but tedious when it came to trailing him.

He lived in a neighborhood on a hill overlooking the freeway. It looked like it should have a gated entry, but Hart figured it was either built before people such as the assemblyman started scaring people into believing gates were necessary, or the developers did their homework and realized they could save some construction costs by sparing an unnecessary feature.

Even in the more populated enclaves of the county, crime rates were low. Violent crime was especially rare. When it did happen, it took place in pockets of the region that were nothing like and nowhere near the assemblyman's voters. He always assured his fans that the violence was not decades of racial and economic tension, and denial that any of those things mattered, coming to a bloody juncture. He wanted them to know that violence was caused by lazy people who weren't responsible gun owners.

Hart watched his home from down the street. He had some excuses and props ready for nosy neighbors, but people hardly came out of their houses. It may have been too late in the afternoon. The sun was at its highest point, and the wind blew hardest at this hour. People had already taken their walks or washed their cars or groomed their front yards. They were inside resting, including the assemblyman's wife. He knew she was in there. She had been onstage at the rally, and they came home together after the fundraiser luncheon at the Best Western courtyard atrium.

It was probably foolish to think she would do anything but rest after such a full afternoon, but Hart thought maybe she would also need to run some errands now that she had the chance.

One of the three doors of their garage opened, and a luxury car backed out. She was at the wheel, driving solo.

Hart leaned over to reach for something out of the glove compartment as she passed. He pulled out a pair of wire-rimmed reading glasses and a souvenir canvas baseball cap from Yosemite National Park. They were meant to compliment his fleece vest, flannel shirt, and the spacious jeans he wore when working in the garden. If there was any doubt as to whether he was non-threatening, the sandals he wore over thick gray sweat socks would alleviate any fear. He grabbed a clipboard bursting with frayed papers from under his seat, then hung a lanyard around his neck with a vague permit slid inside the plastic license holder that dangled from it.

"What did you say the name of your group was?" the assemblyman asked as Hart stood in his doorway holding the clipboard and a meek smile.

"We're new."

"I didn't think there could possibly be an anti-gun 501c that I hadn't heard of."

"Oh, I see you're quite familiar with the world of non-profits."

"You don't know who I am?"

"Someone concerned about gun violence, I hope."

"I am," the assemblyman smiled. "But we probably have different views on how to stop it."

"Do you work for a gun lobby?"

The assemblyman burst out laughing.

"I've been accused of that."

Hart smiled politely and betrayed nothing.

"Wayne Raine," the assemblyman held out his hand. "State Assembly, Sixteenth District."

"Ah," Hart performed an act of recognition. "Of course. 'Make It Wayne, Make It Rain.'"

"That's me."

"Well, this is certainly embarrassing. Here I am canvassing for a political issue, and I don't even recognize my local politician."

"That's okay," Raine patted him on the arm, switching to campaign mode. "But I'm surprised they don't have my picture on a dart board at your headquarters."

"I wouldn't know," Hart shrugged. "I'm very new at this myself. I just recently decided I wanted to get involved."

"And why is that?"

Hart said the name of Stanley's elementary school.

Raine put on a weighty expression he wore a little too well. He resembled a news anchor making the transition from a story about puppy adoptions to a vehicular manslaughter.

"That incident shook us all," Raine captioned his look.

"Some more than others," Hart had to try harder to stay in character. He focused on the sadness rather than the anger.

"Did you know someone involved?"

"A good friend of mine..."

Hart couldn't finish the sentence. The friend was supposed to be the grandfather of one of the children. That was going to be the story. But as soon as he started to say it out loud, he thought of what a good little friend Stanley had been. He enjoyed spending time with him more than anyone else he could recall.

"Would you like to come inside?" Raine offered. "Rest awhile?"

The assemblyman's façade appeared to chip.

"Thank you," Hart accepted his invitation.

"Have a seat," Raine gestured to the sofa as he closed the door behind them. "Can I get you something to drink? Water? Juice?"

"You're very kind," Hart sat down. "But this is already above and beyond."

"It's really no trouble."

Hart didn't want to leave any fingerprints.

"I'm fine, Mr. Raine. Really."

"Please," Raine sat on the adjoining sofa. "Call me Wayne."

"I'm Allan."

Hart decided he should use fresh names for each mission. Using BC every time was manageable when he was the investigator, but now he was the investigated, and he needed variety.

"I appreciate a man of conviction, even if I may disagree with him," Raine announced. Then, to prove his point, he leaned in and said more softly, "I'd like to make a donation in the name of your friend's child."

"Grandchild, actually."

"Grandchild," Raine reflected on the word.

"That's very kind of you, sir. But I think they would prefer some movement on gun safety regulations a lot more."

Raine exhaled and bowed his head before popping back into their conversation.

"Wouldn't we all?" he offered.

"I'll take that as a 'no.'"

"I have to represent my constituents," Raine lectured. "And I have some very devoted gun owners in that constituency."

"Some," Hart focused on the qualifier.

"The key word isn't 'some,'" he clung to his campaign personae. "It's 'devoted.'"

"I understand they're a vocal group, Wayne," Hart took him up on the invitation to use his first name, trying to dig the man out from under his image. "But they're not a large group."

"Gun owners? Not a large group?"

"Come on, Wayne. You know who I'm talking about. You're the one who used the word 'devoted'. The uncompromising ones. The fanatics. Most gun owners are perfectly okay with some reasonable measures."

"Until the zealots get to them. They sense a change in the weather, and they break out the rain dances and virgin sacrifices."

"You're really scared of them."

"Scared?" Raine didn't like that word, as Hart expected. "Concerned, maybe."

"You said you admire people of conviction. Do you not hold yourself to that same standard?"

"Absolutely I do."

"Then you must agree with them. You must be as radical as they are."

"It's not radical," Raine snapped. "It's in the Constitution."

Hart pulled back. He was proud of shaking the politician out of him, but being too aggressive was out of character for the role Hart was playing.

"How many guns do you have?" he softened his tone.

Hart was genuinely curious, and wanted to make this all about Wayne, who chuckled modestly.

"You'll probably storm out," he said.

"I can handle it," Hart prodded him. "This is what a free society is all about. Civil discourse."

"It's about something else, too."

Raine stood up and gestured for Hart to follow him down the hall.

They entered his home office, which consisted of a desk in one corner, and hundreds of guns everywhere else. They were packed into racks, enough to pass for a gun dealer showroom, far surpassing the number Hart had in mind.

"It looks like the prop room for a Terminator movie," he marveled.

"Only these aren't props," Raine smacked the closest rack.

"How did you get here?"

"What do you mean?"

"Your feelings about guns."

"Well, like I said..."

"And don't mention the Constitution. Everyone knows what it says, more or less. People hear words or read words and decide to like them or hate them because of who they are. How did guns become such an important part of you?"

"They were always around," Raine played along, but not at full speed.

"Lots of people grow up around guns. They don't all become so captivated by them."

"Captivated?"

"Sorry," Hart conceded. "But I'm trying to understand. Why would you be such a fan of something that causes so much misery?"

"They're not dangerous if you know how to use them."

"Knowing how to use them also means you can cause a lot of damage."

"Depending on the person."

"Exactly," Hart took a step in his direction. "So why allow any kind of person access? Why risk a madman getting his hands on one just so you can have an easier time getting one?"

"Safety."

"Safety..."

"Look at it this way," Raine briefly touched Hart's arm. "Some kids get autism from vaccinations, but it's worth it to make sure we keep certain diseases away. The concerns of the millions outweigh those of the few."

"Vaccines don't cause autism."

"Maybe not. I'm just saying even if they did, it wouldn't matter."

"It's not just a few lives ruined by guns every year. Every day, for that matter."

"Relative to the safety they provide for millions, I'm afraid it is a few."

"When immunizations go up, diseases goes down. When guns go up, gun deaths go up with it."

"Again, it's relative. Take away guns, violence still happens."

"But with more effort, more difficulty. Guns make violence easier and more lethal."

"Guns make prevention easier, too. They're a deterrent."

They were back to the kind of debate that carousels with no resolution. Hart needed to bring it back to the personal. Everything is personal, he reminded himself, but everyone wants to pretend it isn't. Everyone wants to be the logical one, and the logical one doesn't exist.

"I guess you've never had any bad experiences with guns," he said.

Raine straightened up.

"My favorite uncle committed suicide when I was a teenager."

He said it as though he had therefore won the argument.

"I'm sorry," Hart said.

"I loved my uncle," Raine tempered his enthusiasm. "But he was weak."

"And I suppose you think he would have done it even if he didn't have a gun."

"He tried to hang himself. He tried pills."

"And they didn't work."

"I know what you're getting at."

"Did you find him?"

"No."

"Have you seen anyone with a gunshot wound? Had to identify anyone who's been shot to death?"

"Have you?"

"Yes," Hart nearly told him the truth. "Oh, yes."

He looked at the display of guns. The top level, the bottom level. The guns mounted on the walls. Raine watched him look, then turned to take in the view as well. The triggers, the grips, the barrels, the muzzles.

"I would never," he said to Hart as they stood and stared at the firepower. "And I mean never, ever, use these to harm innocent life."

"How do you know?"

"I know what I'm doing. And I'm of sound mind."

"Currently."

"I am not my uncle."

He turned to face Hart, positioning himself in front of his arsenal.

"You must have seen the stats," Hart said. "One of these guns is far more likely to kill you, or someone you love, rather than any intruder, whoever you imagine them to be."

"I don't agree."

"Now multiply that by the number of guns in this room, Wayne, and you're practically signing your own death certificate."

"If you believe those studies."

Hart hesitated. He needed to get them off the merry-go-round again.

"Was it really your uncle?" he asked Raine.

"I beg your pardon ?

"Uncle is one of those fallback titles. Uncles are the dog that ate your homework."

"What if it wasn't?"

"None of my business," Hart said, then gestured to the racks behind Wayne. "I'm just wondering how many times over you have to prove you're not like him."

"They're for defending my home."

"Who are you expecting to attack you? North Korea?"

"History is piled with the dead bodies of citizens not allowed to defend themselves."

"And if this video game comes to life, what happens to all of these weapons? Are you raising a militia?"

"I'll do whatever it takes. I'm not the naïve one here."

"What if they get into the wrong hands?"

"I was under the impression you didn't think the world would ever come to that."

"Your room is not the last stop for these machines, no matter what happens. They're going to outlive you."

"Was it really your friend's grandson?"

Hart was stunned. He didn't anticipate Wayne getting personal, but was delighted that he had. Hart decided to pay him back with all the honesty he could afford.

He shook his head.

"Was it your grandson?" Wayne asked.

Hart nodded.

The assemblyman sighed.

"All politics is personal," he said.

Hart picked up on it.

"I couldn't agree more."

"Look at that," Wayne flapped his hand back and forth between them. "Agreement."

"Human beings," Hart shrugged. "We're funny."

Wayne turned to take stock of his collection. He looked as though he was taking in a sunset.

"I've lost a lot of battles these past several years," he said. "Pretty much every social issue. I could always rely on guns for a victory."

"You still can," Hart felt like he had a chance. "And not just on behalf of the loud. You can be a hero to a larger, more sensible group."

Wayne pulled his glance away from his guns, and looked at Hart.

"I'll see what I can do," he said.

Hart wanted to hug him.

Wayne appeared to strike up a conversation with himself.

"There must be something that can make a dent without getting me tarred and feathered."

"We'll have your back."

Wayne wasn't encouraged. Hart tried harder.

"There's a level-headed majority thirsting for leadership on this issue, Wayne. You can be that leader."

"I'll look into the options," he appeared slightly more emboldened. "Take the temperature of each. Background checks, wait periods, registries..."

He peeked at his guns.

"Well, maybe not a registry. But who knows? There's bound to be one I can convince them isn't a deal with the devil."

Hart thanked him as rigorously as he shook his hand.

As he walked out the door, he considered keeping up his fake identity by walking toward the neighbor's house, but Raine didn't linger in his doorway for long.

When he heard the door shut, Hart jumped in the air and pumped a fist. Even if he was a canvasser, he wouldn't need to go to any more homes. He had the ear of a state assemblyman.

He took Peaches to a rally for Wayne Raine at a park in the downtown area. Megan was out of town, otherwise he would have invited her, too. He texted her instead, and suggested she keep an eye on the Raine campaign. Hart wished she was there with them. It would have been a perfect time to introduce Megan and Peaches. A county supervisor served as the warm-up act. Before introducing Raine, she made a speech that could have suggested the county secede and form its own state, and Hart would not have heard a word. He was too busy imagining what this turning point meant for all of them. For Megan, for Quentin, and by extension, even Peaches.

But Raine didn't fulfill his promise, or at least give any indication that anything had changed. He took the stage and resorted to his usual bluster. They were coming for our guns. They were coming for our freedom. Guns and freedom. Freedom and guns. Guns and freedom and freedom and guns. No guns, no freedom. They hate guns because they hate freedom. We love guns because we love freedom. Never mind the well-regulated militia. Load up!

"Why are we here?" Peaches asked Hart as Raine moved on to the subject of moral decay.

"Sorry," he kissed her. "I was just curious."

They strolled away from the gathering and found a restaurant where they only had to wait five minutes for a table.

Hart immersed himself in his phone to hide his despondency. He texted Megan. "Never mind," he told her. He scanned Raine's website, he searched for news items associated with his name. There was no sense of their conversation ever happening.

It was easy enough to shelter his detachment while they stood waiting, but once they were seated, the degree of difficulty climbed.

"Are you okay?" Peaches wasn't fooled by his phone.

"Just concentrating."

"It must be hard hearing someone talk about guns that way."

Hart came out from behind his screen.

"I tried to understand," he said. "I thought if I knew why they feel the way they do, then I could figure out a way to change their minds."

"Why are you talking about it in the past tense?"

"Because I found out it's impossible."

"Nonsense," she scolded him. "Only the best tacticians bother trying to understand their enemy. You're already onto something."

"Enemy..." Hart pondered aloud.

"Opponent," Peaches corrected herself.

"No, you're right. Enemies must be fought, must be defeated, must surrender. That's exactly how this works."

"Hart," she reached across the table. "I know you're upset. But the tide will turn. Enough people get it."

"Not the people who need to get it."

He asked her about her work. Her job always provided a great way to change the subject. She talked about how many of her patients don't notice much about the world around them. They are too absorbed in the struggle within themselves, battling their bodies, their minds caught in the fray.

She noticed the Yosemite ball cap in the backseat of his car.

"We should go there sometime," she said.

"That would be nice," he agreed.

As he waited down the street from Raine's house, he held the cap in his hand, running his fingers over the stitching. The letters that spelled the name, the depiction of Half Dome, of El Capitan, of The Three Brothers rising from the valley. He pictured a trip there with Peaches. She was the type who would like to pitch a tent and hike constantly. To train for it, maybe he could convince Nando to take some hills with him, walk up the gravel roads that branched out from the street they usually walked that marked the city limits. Maybe even wander off the paths into the meadows that lifted into the horizon and held up the silhouettes of oak trees.

Raine's wife backed out of the garage.

Hart put on the cap, and then the glasses to complete the costume he wore last time, but with one addition.

He felt for the pair of surgical gloves in his pocket as he knocked on Raine's door.

CHAPTER 10

The photograph stayed on the assemblyman's social media page for no more than fifteen minutes before someone from his staff took it down.

That was enough time.

Someone captured it and posted it on their page. By the time Raine's office demanded that person remove it, the photo had taken on a life of its own. Few people saw it. A sense of decorum and taste prevented them. But everyone heard about it.

A state assemblyman was dead from a gunshot wound, lying in front of his enormous gun collection. The caption read, "Guns don't love you back," followed by the hashtags #moregunsmoredeath and #whatgunsdo.

The two hashtags were to provide options. If one didn't take off, perhaps the other would. But each faction adopted one as their own. The anti-gun team used "more guns more death", while the pro-gun club claimed "what guns do", using it to post stories of people defending themselves, pictures of families shooting together, and articles discussing where guns are boosting local economies. Hart's intention was for people to post more grisly photos in the spirit of the one he took, which wasn't happening on the anti-gun hashtag, either. They were sharing studies and statistics supporting the theory that was the basis for the "more guns more death" title. They aimed at the head, not the gut. And the head is harder to hit.

Hart cut himself some slack over neither hashtag working out the way he had planned. The photo wasn't planned, and the hashtags consequently created in haste.

Raine was holding his phone when Hart shot him.

Hart tapped on the social media icon, and the assemblyman's page opened, no password required. He took the picture and looked out the window before posting it, making sure no one was outside to see him exit.

No one had seen him enter, either.

When Raine answered the door, Hart asked him why he didn't follow through on his word. Raine was incredulous.

"I'm just glad I found out your organization was a fake before I did anything," he scoffed. "Is your name even Allan?"

"No."

"What about this grandchild of yours? Is that bullshit, too?"

Hart gave him a look that had the assemblyman raising his hands in apology.

"Forgive me," Raine said. "So why the charade?"

"I didn't think I could get a meeting with you. I figured you've had enough family members from the school in your face."

Raine rolled his eyes.

"See?" Hart called him on it. "Is my point any less valid than it was last week?"

"You had no right to make your point the way you did."

Hart had to get inside and off the front step.

"My methods may be extreme," he bowed his head. "I admit that. And I'm sorry. But I need something to happen. We do the same thing over and over and over. It's a bad dream. I lost the only person I truly knew. My grandson wasn't mysterious yet. He hadn't reached that age. I had forgotten how beautiful it is to really know someone. My daughter's grown up and full of surprises now. But her boy, that gorgeous soul. I knew that person."

Raine nodded and nearly smiled.

"I have a granddaughter with one of those cute little-kid speech impediments," he said. "She can't say my name. Can't pronounce her r's. She sees one of my posters and yells 'Wayne Wayne.'"

"It's the small moments," Hart agreed. "That's what I miss the most. I don't remember them until something triggers them. A sound, an object, a song. Then this little piece of time comes back that meant nothing, and now it means everything."

He almost showed him his video, but Raine was lost in contemplation, and Hart didn't want to interrupt.

"I can't imagine," Raine pulled himself out of his thoughts.

"It's like having a gambling addiction forced on you," Hart rode the momentum. "I lost everything, and everyone keeps telling me the only way to get it back is to keep gambling. It's hell. It's the very definition of hell."

"You want a bottle of water or something?" Raine asked.

"That would be great."

Raine ushered him in. Hart sat on the same couch like last time while his host went to the kitchen and brought out a bottle of water that he set on the coffee table.

Hart didn't reach for it.

"I do appreciate the water, Wayne, but may I also ask for one small, symbolic gesture?"

"What's that?" Raine was skeptical.

"It doesn't involve any legislation."

"Okay..."

"Get rid of one weapon," Hart looked him in the eye. "Just one of the hundreds you have."

Raine shook his head and nearly laughed.

"If I bring a gun to the police station, to some buyback program, it'll be all over the news."

"Let me do it. They take them no questions asked."

"And I'm supposed to trust you?"

"We had something," Hart said. "You offered me the first glimmer of hope I've experienced since the shooting. And yes, it may have been under false pretenses, but what happened was real. And I'm grateful."

Raine sighed.

"All right," he cocked his head in the direction of his office. "Your choice. Nothing from the top rack, though."

Hart spent a minute surveying the guns while Raine administered to his phone. Hart asked to use the bathroom.

Raine glanced up and gave him a "down the hall."

Hart walked past the bathroom to the master bedroom.

As he slid on his gloves, he looked at what was on top of each nightstand. One had a jar of moisturizer and a pair reading glasses. The other had the television remote. He approached the nightstand with the remote and opened the drawer.

A small bottle of aspirin rolled around next to a nine millimeter handgun, partially obscured by a brochure for testosterone therapy.

Hart reached in and pulled the gun.

"Last chance," he muttered to himself as he checked to see if it was loaded.

It was.

He initially looked at Raine's phone to make sure he wasn't in the middle of a text that needed to be finished.

Raine was texting with someone named Mitch.

"U won't believe who showed up at my door."

"That old hippie."

"Bingo."

"What happened?"

"He's still here. Call u later."

"Show that lib pussy who's boss."

The thread seemed to need a last word from Raine.

Hart typed a word and sent it.

"Done."

He was about to put the phone by Raine's side when he got the idea for the picture, then the caption, then the hashtags.

He was about to leave when he saw the bottle of water still on the coffee table. He grabbed it on his way out.

He was thirsty.

He kept the bottle by his bedside, refilling it when empty.

It wasn't the only reminder of what he had done. The illness felt familiar. It had the same symptoms as with Glenn, as though his degree of remorse coincided with how close to home his target lived, a local virus infecting his guilt. The congestion and exhaustion lasted a few days. The aftermath lasted several. His respiratory system felt composed wholly of new skin, as if a scab had been lifted from its entirety. Every inhale, every sip of water made him wince and cough from the sensitivity. He remembered when he was feeling bad about Glenn, how much of that sickness he thought was related to who Glenn was, as each new episode of his sad biography was released. Hart had convinced himself that targeting a more shiny member of the community would cause fewer side effects, as he would feel less like a bully. He moaned out loud, more than once, how wrong he was as he exited his latest coughing fit.

Wayne's story was inescapable. Hart could look up the fallout from his road trips at his convenience. Wayne was everywhere.

People scrawled adoring, uplifting graffiti on his campaign signs that were staked into lawns, and the larger versions strapped to fences and posts in front of businesses. A popular meme developed on the signs that used his slogan, "Make It Wayne, Make It Raine", wherein people would write "tears from heaven" after "Raine". Most simply wrote "Justice for Wayne" at the top or bottom, or "Rest in Peace". Nobody wrote anything disparaging, not on the signs.

Those who reveled in the irony of Wayne's cause of death did so through articles and blogposts, some more indulgently than others. Authors attached to reputable sources used the Raine case as an anecdote they danced with to portray what should be done about guns. The comment threads and social media posts were less diplomatic, mocking how Wayne "died surrounded by loved ones," but were no less convinced they also had answers.

Organizations like Megan's seized the moment as best they could.

"Never let a crisis go to waste," Hart said to Peaches. "I believe that's the old expression."

She had convinced him to get out of the house. He reluctantly agreed to meet her for lunch at a tacqueria downtown. He was feeling better, but paranoid. The hypersensitivity of his insides had him convinced he was vulnerable to bacteria and viruses he would normally fend off. Plus he was enjoying the ability to lie in bed and breathe without coughing.

"Can't say I blame them," she said. "The laws would seem to write themselves after what happened."

"Everybody has examples. We lob them back and forth at each other."

"Like a tennis match."

"Everyone has analogies, too."

Peaches raised her chin and pursed her lips, chiding him for having so many answers.

He grinned in lieu of an apology. He was right, but agreed he sounded like someone who hadn't held a conversation in over a week.

"Nando!" Peaches looked over Hart's shoulder.

He turned to see Nando approach.

"Please don't ask him to join us," Hart said in time for Nando to hear. "Please don't ask him to...oh. Hi, Nando."

"I was already invited, smart ass."

Peaches groaned.

"You couldn't wait?" she said.

"What's going on?" Hart asked.

"This is an intervention," Nando blurted out.

"Good Lord," Peaches collapsed into the back of her chair. "Why did I call you?"

"I'm sure Hart prefers we cut to the chase. Eh, bud?"

"An intervention for what? I don't have an addiction and I'm not in an abusive relationship. At least, I didn't think I was."

He smirked at Peaches.

"They never do," Nando laughed.

Peaches wasn't biting.

"You're not dealing with Stanley's death in a healthy manner," she said.

Hart panicked. Was there a new description of him he hadn't heard about? One that included the Yosemite hat? Peaches saw that hat in his car. Maybe Raine had said something about it to a staffer who had come forward with this new piece of information.

"Her idea," Nando pointed at Peaches.

They weren't acting as though they suspected he was a murderer.

"How am I not dealing with Stanley's death in a healthy manner?"

"You disappear for days on end," she said.

"I was sick."

"You lie to us, play us off each other and leave town with neither of us."

"That's what sold me," Nando explained. "That was weird."

Hart relaxed.

"Where do you go?" Peaches asked.

"I need to get away now and then. What's wrong with that?"

"Why can't you tell us that?"

"I didn't want you to worry. Depressed guy leaving town by himself. I didn't want to tell you 'no' when you inevitably asked to join me. And I do mean you, not Nando. I used him for your sake, then figured, well, I guess I might as well return the favor."

"I'm touched," Nando quipped.

"What's your plan?" Hart asked. "What do you want me to do?"

"Therapy," she said.

"Did it."

"Not enough, obviously."

"Didn't care for it."

"You took a month of mandatory appointments with an assigned grief counselor," Peaches said.

"How did you find that out?"

"I'm a doctor, and I make friends quickly."

"So I'll bet you know some really great therapist."

"I most certainly do…"

She reached inside her bag for a business card which she handed to Hart, who scowled at it.

"She'll give you a free consultation," she pitched. "Her name is Andrea. But you can call her Dr. Sands."

"And let me guess, she's going to conclude that I need to see her as often as possible."

"Think about it. Please."

"And while you're thinking about it," Nando jumped back in. "Come with me next weekend for real. There's a law enforcement convention up north."

"Full of cops and ex-cops in therapy."

"I told you he'd see right through it," Nando said to Peaches.

"I'll go, Nando," he surrendered. "I'll go. Just let me hit the free consultation first. That way when one of your buddies at the convention talks to me about therapy, I can honestly say I'm trying it."

"And maybe you'll be able to say you like it," Peaches tried.

Hart hung his eyes at her and sighed.

"Or at least appreciate it," she offered.

Dr. Sands was nice enough.

"Though who ever heard of a nasty therapist?" Hart speculated out loud during their session.

"You may be surprised."

"Oh, come on…"

"Some people like a harsh approach. And if they're being billed by the hour, they're going to go with what they like."

"Sounds more like entertainment than therapy," Hart said.

"It's consumer-driven, like any market."

"What about what they need?"

"What about what you need?" Dr. Sands smiled.

"You're probably used to people trying to avoid the subject."

"Very used to it."

"I don't know where to start. Can you ask me questions?"

"Are you afraid of loud noises?"

"No."

"Crowds?"

"Nope."

"Do you find yourself mapping out exit routes in public places? Keeping an eye on people you find suspicious?"

"I don't have PTSD. My career was low-key. I was never the first one through the door. And I wasn't in the room with Stanley when it happened. I wasn't there. If he survived, I'm sure he would have it."

"I'm trying to find something to focus on."

"It's not fear. Any fears I had disappeared with Stanley. I used to love being in public places with him. My favorite thing to do with him was go to this diner downtown, that old joint that's been there since before this place became a destination. We'd go there after school, between the lunch and dinner rush, in the middle of the afternoon. The other kids and their families would go to the frozen yogurt place or for smoothies. We'd split a slice of pie and talk like a couple of old men. The place to ourselves, just us and the waitress who called us both 'sweetie.'"

He paused. He had to.

"So I'm not scared when I find myself at a table in that diner, or anywhere else for that matter. I'm sad. And if someone did come in and start shooting, I wouldn't hesitate to rush him."

"A chance at redemption?"

"A chance to stop feeling sad."

"Is that something you think about often?"

"Stopping a shooter?"

"Sacrificing yourself."

"I didn't say anything about sacrificing myself."

"It's the most likely outcome."

"I'm not suicidal."

"You said you're terribly sad and dream of rushing someone firing a gun."

"I didn't say I dream about it."

"It implies you feel you have nothing to lose."

"You know what I do dream about?"

"What?"

"Having a purpose."

"You're lacking one?"

"No," Hart was adamant. "I have one. But it's out of reach."

"Something about making sure what happened to your grandson doesn't happen to anyone else."

"Something like that."

"And taking out a shooter would be a tangible accomplishment."

"Sure."

"There are other ways to help."

"More realistic ways?" he read her mind with a sidelong look.

"You said it," she smiled. "Not me."

"There is nothing realistic about any of it. The whole scene is pure emotion. Two gangs of toddlers screaming at each other."

"I can see why you're sad."

"Can you see why I believe that?"

"I don't know enough about it."

"Thank you for admitting that."

"But there's always a solution."

"Ah, Dr. Sands..."

"Hart..."

"You almost had me, Dr. Sands."

"What would be the point of you coming back if you honestly feel there is no point?"

"I could express my frustration, talk about the futility of it all, get things off my chest."

"I'm solutions-oriented."

"Sounds like the motto of a consulting firm."

"I thought someone with your background would appreciate a pragmatic approach."

"A law and order guy."

"I wouldn't peg you as wanting to talk for talk's sake."

"Even if I told you I have no one to talk to?"

"No one?"

"I talk a little bit to Peaches. But I don't want to burden her. And those who went through it, don't want to talk about it."

Dr. Sands shifted in her seat and appeared to use the time to reconsider her position.

"If you just want to talk," she said, "Okay."

"The customer's always right."

"Not sure I'd go that far. But they do know what they want."

The session wasn't a full hour. That only happened for the full price.

He gave her his insurance information so she could see how many, if any, upcoming hours would be covered.

He wasn't sure he wanted to attend any more, but the insurance card offered him a chance to stall, and if he decided against it, he wouldn't have to tell her in person.

Their exchange about customers being right, or at least certain, came to mind while he was strolling through the law enforcement convention with Nando. He had wandered off on his own and found himself in the hubbub of the merchant hall.

He chatted up two sales reps who anchored a booth for a firm that referred to itself as being in the business of home defense. They didn't display any firearms. Instead they brandished their capacity to accessorize gun owners with all the trimmings, whether the consumer wanted an urban commando look, or more of a country militia vibe.

"It's too late to compete with the old guard when it comes to guns," one of them said.

Aside from one rep being to his left, and one to his right, Hart had a hard time telling them apart. They both wore company polo shirts, dark green with a gray logo on their chests, a wolf head facing forward, nose down, eyes glaring upward, teeth bared.

"Jumping in against the big boys would be corporate suicide," said the other. "It would be like starting a new company that drills for oil, or makes cars, or jumbo jets."

"We are a licensed firearms dealer, but that's not our bread and butter."

"Think of all the money that was made during the gold rush by people who weren't mining for gold," each played off the other seamlessly. "The people who sold the miners their jeans, hats, and bandanas. What we do is bring some style to the business. Some flair."

"I grew up on the whole Soldier of Fortune thing, and still love it, but it's limiting. There's a bigger audience out there."

"Like how Apple made computers into fashion statements."

"But they actually make computers," Hart reminded them.

"True," one acknowledged. "But look at the businesses they inspired."

"Cases, apps."

" And we do make weaponry."

"Or at least put our name on some."

"Just not traditional firearms."

"Stun guns, tasers."

"If you don't want to shoot to kill, we can help. If you want to shoot to kill, and feel safer doing it..."

"Or look good doing it..."

"We can help you there, too."

"Holsters, bullet proof vests, camo, attachments for your weapons, accessories..."

"Speaking of which..." one of them reached under the table for a coffee mug. "This is a new line of schwag we came up with ourselves. Check it out. You know that old gag where you say 'That's what she said' after any sentence, or 'In bed'?"

"Sure," Hart shrugged.

"We've invented our own version of that."

He held up the mug, which read *World's Greatest Dad...*, then turned it around to reveal the other side, which read, *...With an AR-15.*

Hart conjured up a polite smile.

"The beauty of it is we can rehash any old cliché and attach our spin to the end, then put it on any piece of merchandise."

"Hang On, Baby, Friday's Coming...With an AR-15."

"I'd Rather Be Sailing...With an AR-15."

"Just Do It...With an AR-15."

"Nike may come after you on that one," Hart said.

Both of the reps laughed.

"No doubt," one said. "But you get the idea."

"And we can of course use different types of guns. It doesn't have to be the AR-15. Whatever the customer wants. We'll customize it."

"It adds some fun to what we do. We're still a home defense firm at heart. We sell alarm systems, panic room schemas, doomsday supplies. People come to us because they're scared. Putting on a friendly face helps us reach them on another level."

"The competition is too obvious when it comes to the fear factor. The commercials with the scary synthesizer music and the actors in hoodies rushing the door or putting their fist through the window."

"Guys in ski masks swinging crowbars."

"Fear is easy."

"We have a slogan," one said.

"More of an expression," the other corrected him. "We'd never put it on a business card."

"Oh yeah?" Hart was intrigued.

"Stoke more fear, sell more gear."

"More fear, more gear. That's the short version."

"Our challenge, as we see it, is to emphasize comfort."

"Camouflage the fear," Hart said.

"Hey," one of them said while the other made a whistling face. "We may have to borrow that."

"With an AR-15," Hart added.

The reps laughed.

They laughed for quite a while.

Hart nodded along.

When they were finished, he thanked them for their time, then moved down the aisle, surveying the other booths. As he walked through the massive event center, past the merchants who filled it, he thought more deeply about something he had thought about since his time with the assemblyman.

It was easy to characterize politicians like Wayne as sales reps as well, but they still enjoyed guns, and weren't completely for sale. Contributions were a bonus. Wayne never expressed any concern over corporate interests, at least not in their conversations. His hesitation had been grounded in the voices of his loudest constituents. And Wayne's anxieties were genuine, as far as Hart could tell. But where did the anger in his voters' volume come from? Perhaps it wasn't the politicians who were being manipulated by firearm companies. It was the public, who then pressured their politicians.

Either way, it was fair to say that people like the ones he met at the convention bore some responsibility. Hart assumed the owners and board members of the largest gun producers would be near-impossible targets, and so concluded that a smaller firm like the Wolf shirts would be a more efficient way to further develop his message.

He walked through the rest of the convention with his new mission on his mind. Not only on the floor of the event center, but in the ballrooms of the hotel where he and Nando stayed, and the lunches and dinners they attended. He held half-hearted conversations with the old cops Nando introduced him to.

Nando noticed and added those interactions to his evidence that Hart was still reeling from Stanley.

"That will never stop," Hart told him as they lay on their beds in the hotel room watching sports highlights on their last night before heading home.

Nando didn't respond. Not for a while.

He hooted and grunted at some of the plays that unfolded on the screen before asking Hart a question.

"Did you recognize anyone here?"

"What, like any cops or pensioners?"

"Yeah. You run into anybody?"

"No."

Nando said "Hmm," and let it trail into silence.

Hart knew it was bait. He took some time to decide how much he cared about what was on Nando's mind.

"Why do you ask?" he tugged on the line.

"I was thinking maybe you were always this way."

"This way?"

"You know. Depressed."

"Because I don't recognize anyone in a crowd of broken-down old cops?"

"This convention is huge. The biggest in the state. The western region, probably."

"I have a friend in New York City. I don't expect to run into him there unless I call."

"Is there anyone you can call here?"

"I preferred not to take my work home with me."

"Did you make even one friend on the force?"

"I didn't have a lot friends, period."

"Well, there ya go."

Hart waited to respond. He didn't want to sound too defensive.

"Some depressed people surround themselves with friends to avoid facing their problems."

"And you're the other type."

"This is why I hate cops," Hart spat. "Fucking know-it-alls. A simple answer for everything. Everything is black and white."

Nando chuckled.

Hart laughed, too, while wishing he wasn't.

"And you are Exhibit A," he tried to stay focused on his anger at Nando.

"You were in the wrong business."

"Maybe I was."

"Why did you become a cop?"

"Maybe the job changed me."

"You're saying 'maybe' a lot."

"Because I don't know, Nando. I don't know. Nothing happened on the job. There was no single event, some big story I can tell that changed everything. Sure, shit happened. Shitty shit. But mostly the world just kept spinning, and I grew more aware of it. Every passing day. And if the job didn't help me see the world for what it is, then...well, you know. Other things did."

Hart had sometimes wondered if it was possible to shut Nando up. He had succeeded.

Perhaps too well. Nando had never seemed so unsure of himself. The one-liners were missing from the rest of their stay, and the drive home.

Even their first walk the morning after they arrived was stilted, nearly absent of quips. When Nando attempted one, his delivery was unsteady. He was aiming rather than firing. Hart vacillated between feeling guilty and indifferent. Indifference started to take the lead as he considered how much of a friend Nando could have been if he was that unaware of Hart's condition up until then. Hart wondered whether that ignorance had been willful or blissful.

Nando stopped showing up to walk with him. The first time, he called with an excuse about his knee bothering him. The next day he had plans with his wife.

Then he stopped calling.

Hart thought it was for the best. If he was going to work his way up the gun hierarchy, the missions would become more risky. When the risk caught up with him, he wanted to leave as few grieving people behind as possible.

He considered calling Quentin for help with pursuing the CEO of the security firm he glad-handed at the convention. He thought Quentin may know someone who helped them with their online presence. And if he didn't, he could probably still gather some intelligence on them. Involving Quentin would involve dropping any pretense. He would be confessing, forcing Quentin to decide between turning him in or being an accomplice. He would make it clear that Megan wasn't to be included. She would remain in denial.

If his involvement was necessary. Hart did some legwork of his own to gauge the need.

The company's headquarters was listed as a PO Box, with a brick-and-mortar store location advertised in the same city. It was a half-day's drive. He chose a day sandwiched in the midst of a double shift Peaches was scheduled to pull, then set out to assess the situation.

The storefront was modest, standing on a side street two blocks off the main thoroughfare of the business district, a part of town people rolled through to find free parallel parking.

Appearances meant nothing. His career taught him that humble spaces are often used to disguise dubious cash flow.

When the number of hours he staked out the place exceeded the number of people who visited it, he decided to take a look inside.

The wares appeared to be identical to what had been on display in their booth at the convention, and not much more of it. The only addition was the guns on display, locked behind the counter. There was a single employee in front of the guns, a young man reminiscent of the sales reps, but not as glossy. He served as sales associate, cashier, and security consultant.

After a nonchalant lap around the aisles, Hart approached the lone worker.

"Slow day?" Hart asked.

"Pretty typical," he admitted.

"How do you guys make it?"

"Online. About ninety percent of our business is online."

"Why bother with the store?"

"The guns, mainly. Our owner prefers to sell those face-to-face. Plus he thinks it legitimizes the company. He's sold on the idea that people are jittery about small businesses that are strictly on the web. Like there's no accountability. Nobody to complain to if something doesn't work."

"And you disagree?"

"I guess that may be true for older people."

The employee didn't seem to notice or care that his statement may offend someone of Hart's age, which Hart appreciated.

"Then I guess I'm here to prove your point," he said.

The employee became aware of Hart's age and relieved about his reaction all at once.

"The age divide is breaking down, though," he offered something of an apology. "Everyone's adjusting to the new world, even if they didn't grow up in it."

"Have you talked to the owner about this?"

"There may be some value in keeping the store," he shrugged. "Like for security consultations. Even then, we tend to make those appointments online and arrange a home visit."

"So you haven't," Hart teased him.

"I'm still kind of new."

"Probably not much opportunity, anyway."

"Actually I see him pretty much every shift."

"Oh yeah?"

"He likes to visit. Very hands-on. I'm surprised he hasn't come in today."

"Still might?"

"Probably will. If you want to talk to him about something, I can check."

He held up his phone.

"No, I'm good. Just looking for a gift for a friend."

Hart reached for a mesh baseball cap that read, *Don't Worry, Be Happy...With an AR-15*.

"I'll take this."

"We can put that on something else for you. A license plate holder, t-shirt..."

"Coffee mug?"

"You bet. Can change the gun, too."

"This will do."

Hart returned to his car and resumed his stakeout.

The owner showed up within the next half hour.

He walked out from the driveway at the edge of the block of storefronts. Hart wasn't sure it was him at first, but gathered it was upon seeing the way he and the cashier interacted through the front window. The owner had opinions. The employee agreed with them.

Hart hadn't seen a car pull into the back lot through that driveway. There was another access point nearby. When the owner left, Hart pulled into the driveway in time to see him back out of his parking spot in a gray Toyota Camry. Maybe he did pull in through the same driveway, and Hart hadn't noticed. It wasn't the kind of vehicle he was expecting. He reminded himself again how savvy the devious can be when it comes to appearances, and was glad to see there really was another driveway on the opposite end of the lot leading into the next street over.

He trailed him to a cluster of light brown condominiums with dark brown beams of wood accenting its boxiness. It may have been the nicest in town thirty years earlier, but had been surpassed in design, upkeep, and price.

The CEO of the security firm walked across a dried lawn peppered with Big Wheels and plastic playhouses, then climbed some cement slatted stairs that rose above a pile of aluminum cans and beer bottles. Hart thought perhaps the owner was there for a security consultation, but the man drew his keys from his pocket and let himself into the unit at the top of the stairs, the surface of the door bubbled from weather and peeling paint.

Hart was relieved he hadn't contacted Quentin. If he was going to pull him in, make him own his idea after all, Hart wanted it to matter.

He pulled away from the withered condos, left the CEO to his novelty mugs and personalized shoulder holsters, and drove home.

He found a can of soup in his cupboard and heated it up in the microwave. He forgot to cover the bowl with a paper towel or plastic wrap. His mind was elsewhere. He wiped the splatter from the oven walls and window, then sat at the table eating what was left, debating whether he should catch up to where his mind was racing.

His conscience could not hold much longer. It was teeming with more responsibility than it could manage. So much damage had been done. He needed it to mean something.

He needed to think big.

He called Quentin.

CHAPTER 11

"No family members."

"It isn't what you think," Quentin said.

"Especially no children."

"He's an adult."

"I mean children as in sons and daughters. They'll always be children to their parents."

"He's hardly an innocent bystander."

"Megan hinted at this in that conversation we had, this idea of going after family, and I'm not saying I didn't think about it."

"He's a wastrel."

"I'm not being self-righteous."

"Here…"

Quentin took out his phone and started tapping the screen.

"It just feels wrong," Hart said, ignoring what Quentin was doing.

"Look…"

Quentin held up the phone to Hart's face.

"This," he said. "This is the son."

On the screen was a picture of a sunburned youngish man lounging poolside in a bathing suit, a .357 revolver in his lap, and a nude woman on all fours next to him serving as a table, upon which he rested a glass of whiskey-colored liquid on the rocks.

"This is the heir to the fortune," Quentin narrated. "A fortune made on the lives of dead children."

"That's an oversimplification," Hart resisted.

"Does this man strike you as someone interested in nuance? Would he listen to a complex argument about anything? Much less the family business?"

"How involved is he in the business?"

"As far as the day-to-day drudgery goes, I'd be surprised if he knew how to open a spreadsheet, much less read one. But as you can see, he's deeply involved in promotion."

He handed his phone to Hart, who scrolled through the heir's wall of social media.

The posts were of a piece with the one Quentin had shown him. Each photo had at least one woman and one gun in it. The women were hardly clothed, if at all. The guns were all high caliber, capable of doing a gruesome amount of damage. The captions he wrote used "fucking" before almost every verb or adjective, replaced almost every noun with "shit", unless the noun was "woman", which was usually replaced with "bitch", or some epithet that exceeded it for shock value.

Then Hart noticed every post had millions of hits, and thought maybe there was no shock value for his followers. It's how they talked.

"I would say who cares if this guy dies," Hart said. "But it looks like a lot of people would."

"I suspect a lot of those fans are fake accounts, but even if half of them are astroturf, that's still millions who eat his shit up."

Hart glanced at him.

"To use the vernacular," Quentin explained.

"Is he any sort of cautionary tale?" Hart wondered out loud. "Will anyone relate to this guy?"

"He's a dream merchant."

"And you want me to kill those dreams."

"I'm an accessory," Quentin reminded him. "You made sure of that."

Hart ignored Quentin's jab and continued to scroll through the site.

"Plus he's close by," Quentin rebooted his pitch and narrated the photos Hart was looking at. "If he's not in Las Vegas, the party's at his house in the hills above LA. Either way, not far."

"It seems too easy," Hart continued to backpedal. "He fits the pattern I'm trying to move beyond."

"Congressman Gunny Gun?"

Hart lowered the phone.

"The others before him. I need to keep making progress. This guy is the same trash as the dudes selling guns in the parking lot, but with money."

"Money made off of those people. He's an icon to them. If you want to keep making statements, who better?"

Hart sighed.

"Statements nobody hears."

"Are you kidding?" Quentin asked.

"I may have had a purpose in mind, Q, but let's face it. All I've done is kill people. All I've done is contribute to the body count. And since when has a high body count persuaded a gun lover to disarm?"

"You haven't heard?"

"Apparently not."

"I guess Megan couldn't find a way to tell you without compromising herself."

"Tell me what?"

"The copycats."

Hart processed the term.

"Copycats," he tried to make sense of it. "As in people killing the kinds of people I have?"

"Well, not killing per say."

"That's a relief. I guess. So what are they doing?"

"They're lashing out against gun nuts. Defacing their bumper stickers, for example. One person broke the rear window of a pickup truck with a 'Gun Control Means Using Both Hands' sticker on it and made sure to lay the pieces of glass with the sticker on it across the hood."

Hart stared at Quentin.

"I know," Quentin acknowledged Hart's derision. "But it's happening a lot. There's a wave of reports on these kinds of things."

Hart continued to stare.

"I thought you'd be flattered."

"Copycats?"

"You clearly don't want them to kill people."

"Of course not, Q, but come on. No wonder I hadn't seen any of this in the news. They're not stories. They're anecdotes."

"They offer cover."

"I've taken care of my own cover."

"Of course you have, but Megan noticed..."

"Can we keep her out of this?"

"We noticed..."

Hart held up his hand.

"I noticed..."

Hart raised his thumb.

"...These events, big or small, are happening simultaneously at different places. The lone gunman theory is dying."

Hart reared back with surprise.

"There's a lone gunman theory?"

"In some circles."

Hart settled down into silence.

Quentin didn't want to be the one to break it, but enough time passed that he started to wonder if Hart remembered he was there with him.

"I can get us into one of his parties," he said.

Hart looked at him with no particular sign of emotion.

Quentin carried on.

"Some of my colleagues, some friends of mine, know him. As much as the guy loves guns, when it comes to business, he seems more interested in tech. He attends conventions and invests a lot of money with us. I guess it started with him looking for ways to enhance his online presence."

Hart remained indifferent.

Quentin noted that he still held the phone he had handed to him.

"If you keep scrolling," Quentin gestured toward it, "you'll reach his thoughts on school shootings."

Hart glared at him and tossed the phone back.

Quentin caught it.

"Hey," he barked as though the phone had detonated in his hand. "You called me. You pulled me into your rampage."

"You inspired it," Hart reminded him.

"It was still your choice."

"As is the decision whether or not to proceed."

Quentin dropped the phone and stood up.

"So why invite me over?"

"I wanted to see what you had to offer."

"You son of a bitch..."

"So turn me in."

Hart stood up and faced him.

"Turn me in."

Quentin took a breath to gather his thoughts.

"Is that what you want?" he asked.

Hart seemed unsure how to respond.

"Is that all this is?" Quentin pressed.

"It wasn't supposed to be," Hart said.

He sat back down.

"It wasn't the plan."

He looked up at Quentin.

"Believe me."

Quentin sat down as well.

"What's going on, Hart?"

"It's all been so smooth. Everything has worked out perfectly."

He hesitated.

Quentin braced himself for another long pause, but Hart kept it brief this time.

"And not just with the missions, the targets, whatever," he continued. "Regular life has taken this turn for the better. Peaches is wonderful. I couldn't ask for someone I'm more undeserving of. So here we are. A chance at a bright future, but with a talent for avenging the past."

Quentin pocketed his phone and stirred in his seat as though preparing to leave.

"I'm sorry," he said. "I shouldn't have mentioned the lone gunman theory."

Hart eased into a forlorn chuckle.

"Don't leave," he beckoned. "I just didn't realize my chance to get caught was fading."

"There's always that chance," Quentin reminded him.

Hart smiled, trying to make it last longer than he was able.

"Let me know when we're on for the party," he said. "I'll look for an angle to exploit."

Quentin was unsure how to react, as though finally aware of what he had been asking for now that he had it.

"Maybe if I had fallen in love with Peaches before this all started," Hart seemed to say to himself as much as to Quentin. "But it's too late. I forfeited a clean slate. There is no future with a past like mine."

"Think of it as putting others before yourself," Quentin said, as much for his own peace of mind as for Hart's.

"You think I haven't told myself that before?"

Quentin laughed at Hart's comment, but out of obligation. He stopped when it was clear that his laugh was a poor impersonation of one, and he became quite grave instead.

"This isn't some kamikaze mission, is it?" he studied Hart. "A suicide that you're choreographing? Down in a blaze of glory, that sort of thing?"

Hart assured him it was not.

He didn't have to design anything in that regard. It would simply happen, like everything seemed to when it came to this project. He hadn't believed in fate until he had become a lobbyist. An extreme lobbyist. Even the decision to take up such a hobby felt as though it had been made for him.

And as far as the party target was concerned, his research had him convinced that not only was the danger to himself minimal, but he would be able to cajole others to do the job for him.

He read articles about the parties, the presence of loaded weapons around the house that worried the subject's handlers and friends, though whether he had any real friends was a legitimate question as a biography started to emerge. There were people who appeared more often than others in the pictures that accompanied the articles published about him, and in the images he posted on his own site. Hart familiarized himself with their faces, and learned their names when available. Names were more likely among the men. The women remained anonymous, though some were featured rather frequently. A couple were even pictured clothed on occasion, doing something other than shaving him, massaging him, feeding him, or fawning over him in general. Not on his social media feed, naturally, but in random candids that showed up when conducting an image search. They weren't simply models for hire. They were a regular, albeit unnamed, presence.

Hart studied which ones appeared the most, and whom they stood next to mugging for the camera, for it wasn't only the subject they clutched and posed with. There were entourage members who beamed cheek-to-cheek and hip-to-hip more habitually with certain women. Hart hunted for patterns, some of which he knew were merely coincidence, a product of random moments when the photos were snapped. But some were bound to come to life at the party. Some would indeed prove to reflect a certain connection, either realized or unrequited, depending on its potential effect on the subject, the boss, the lord of the party.

When it came to the angles that could be inserted between the vassals who served him, Hart relied on their sunburned leader to drive his research. He tracked his social media posts for issues that were common enough to build a theme, and discovered some he could abuse.

Hart told Peaches he was going to spend some time with Quentin, take a road trip together to strengthen their frayed relationship, all of which was essentially true.

As the date loomed, he assumed the party was going to be cancelled, or moved to Las Vegas, as a brush fire avoided containment in the hills not far from the subject's house. Hart spun some ways he could explain their change of plans to Peaches, but Quentin assured him the party was still on.

"No fire is gonna tell me where I can party!" Quentin imagined how the target may put it.

"Don't you mean 'fucking fire'?" Hart corrected him.

Quentin laughed in agreement as he drove with one arm resting on the open window, winding his luxury car up through the hills of opulence.

Hart was impressed by how calm he appeared. He had framed Quentin's role in simple and safe terms for him.

"Stay away from me once we're in," it went. "Meet me in the car after."

But Quentin was still going to a party where a shooting would happen, and betrayed little concern over it. Hart reckoned that Quentin was taking pride in finally living out the plan he had dreamed up, so he recalibrated his expectations for him. Rather than worry about whether Quentin would be able to go through with it, he worried about his overconfidence. He badgered him about keeping his distance.

"You shouldn't even be able to see me," he emphasized before reaching the part about meeting by the car.

"I know, I know," Quentin gestured. "But I was thinking..."

"Oh boy..."

"We're coming in together, you're my guest, so what difference does it make if we split up? It seems like some kind of standard thing people say in these situations. Or at least the movie versions of these kinds of situations."

"Your name is on the list, mine isn't. It's for your protection. Plausible deniability. Remember?"

"But people will see us. And if not, they'll see on the list that I brought a guest, and someone might ask me about that guest."

"Tell them you don't know me. I'm a venture capitalist from Santa Monica that your company wanted you to bring along to pitch an idea to the party animal once they found out you were going to his house. You picked me up on the way. We met me at some coffee house filled with people on laptops. Take your pick. You know the area better than I do."

Quentin saluted.

The closer they drew to their target, the more they saw helicopters flying with bins of water swinging beneath them, and airplanes growling back and forth to drop and reload fire retardant. The air grew more hazy. Everything appeared to be draped under a thin, dirty cloth. Quentin rolled up his window and looked more hesitant. Few houses were visible, mostly gates and mailboxes, the driveways shrouded in trees and shrubs.

"There are no intersections here," Quentin noted. "Only curves where streets suddenly change names."

They came upon the address, then swung around to find a place to park, which ended up being a quarter-mile and three street names away.

"You'll appreciate the walk on the way back," Hart told him. "Gives you time to settle down."

Quentin nodded, but with no conviction.

His nod before they walked up the stairs to the house was much more determined. He gave their name to the man at the door with the same kind of nonchalance he had possessed during their drive. Hart was reassured, but then disappointed when they walked in and the crowd was smaller than he anticipated.

"It's early," Quentin said. "Wait till the sun goes down."

"We'll see," Hart said.

"You're not thinking of calling it off?" Quentin asked a little too loudly.

Hart silently implored him to lower his voice.

"That's always an option with every mission," he said in a voice intended to demonstrate the proper volume.

"I like how you call it a mission."

"What else would I call it?"

"A job."

"That sounds criminal. At best entrepreneurial. Our work is strictly non-profit."

He tried to give Quentin a reassuring look.

"I'll do my best to see it through," he told him. "Now go mingle."

Quentin obliged and immediately recognized someone. Hart puffed out a light laugh. The subject really did have a lot of tech connections. Quentin stuck to the plan and led his acquaintance to the bar in the next room, while Hart made his way out onto the deck that overlooked the sprawling pool with a half-dozen women sunning themselves around it. He tried to check if he recognized any of them, but was transfixed by a plume of smoke rising from behind a ridgeline two canyons away. It looked like a mushroom cloud from the dropping of an atomic bomb, which made the efforts of the circling planes and helicopters seem feckless.

Hart surveyed the guests to see how many were watching the scene along with him. No one was. He remembered a childhood game that involved staring up at nothing and seeing who joins you, and how much time passes before they realize there is nothing there. He thought since there really was something there this time, something important, the people who noticed along with him might be more sensitive to the world around them, more so than the average guest. And if one of those people who watched the fire with him turned out to be one of the frequent guests he had clocked online, then maybe that person could be the one he used to spark his plan.

"It's kind of beautiful," a young woman's voice remarked.

He looked over to check the source. She was leaning on the railing several paces over, wearing a short robe over a bathing suit. Hart smiled at her and tried to place her, which was complicated by her large sunglasses.

"Weird, I know," she playfully feigned embarrassment. "But it's natural, right? Everyone says, 'ooh, it looks like a bomb dropped,' but it's just nature. It's nature."

She was high. Hart guessed weed, but there were plenty of other options circulating.

"Somebody emptied their Hibachi in the canyon," Hart smiled.

"What?"

"It wasn't caused by natural forces. Just a lazy person cleaning out their grill."

"Yeah," she processed the information. Hart could practically see the neurons slowly firing. "But...it's still fire."

"Can't argue with that."

She laughed some more and said "thank you."

"For what?"

"Not making me feel like an idiot. Well, like more of an idiot than I already feel like."

"I'm sure there's a good reason for that."

"A little weed," she agreed.

"Nature," Hart nodded, proud he had guessed correctly.

She laughed again and introduced herself as Wilma.

"Such an old-fashioned name," he said.

"You were expecting, what, like Trixie? Roxy?"

"Something with an 'x' in it, yeah."

"You're funny. What's your name?"

Hart used the name B.C.

"Talk about old-fashioned," she snorted, then laughed at herself. "How do you know Danny?"

"Tech industry."

"Ah..." she was delighted.

"I'm not rich."

"That's not what I'm here for," she bristled.

"Neither am I."

She appeared to forgive him.

"A lot of girls are," she relaxed again. "I get it. I just reacted that way because I like the tech guys I've met."

"More than the gun guys?"

"They're nice enough. They just have a smaller list of things they like to talk about."

"And how do you know Danny?"

"I'm his favorite."

"Oh, really?"

"Yes," she was aware of how preposterous she sounded. "I'm the one. Why do you think I'm making the rounds? Checking on everyone?"

"You're being a good hostess."

"That's right."

"I thought he was a lucky man thanks to the number of women he has. I didn't realize that number was one."

"Aww."

Hart let the sound of her voice drift off and took in the view, the mushroom cloud and the swimming pool.

"So what are you here for, then?" she restarted their conversation.

"Knives," he kept looking out at the imperiled canyon.

"Knives?"

"I don't like your man's posts about knives. He's always sharing articles about people getting stabbed, attacked by lunatics running amok with knives."

Wilma held onto the railing as she reared back and laughed.

"What?" Hart played innocent. "I'm a knife enthusiast."

"So the pictures of nude women and guns don't bother you, but the knife articles do."

He chuckled along with her before settling down to defend himself.

"You said it yourself," he said. "Us technology guys have a wide variety of interests, and gun guys are more single-minded. They're so protective of their guns, they don't realize the harm they're doing to others."

"Like the knife industry," she still thought it was funny.

"Our weapons have been around since the dawn of civilization. Since the dawn of man, if we're including the pointed stick. We're a link to our heritage, to our primal selves."

"Danny's just showing it's the person, not the weapon."

"I know. I've read the bumper stickers. But no need to pull us into your problems."

Wilma looked at him as though doing so would get her more high.

"And you want to take this up with him?" she finally said.

"Yes."

"Okay," she grinned. "I'll make sure you get the chance."

"Great. Where is he?"

"In bed."

"Not much of a host," he said. "No wonder he needs you."

She expressed her pride in a deep, contented sigh.

"So do those pictures bother you at all?" he asked.

"What pictures?"

"The nude women, the misogynist language."

She continued communicating in sighs, this time an irritated version.

"Let me guess," he narrated her reaction. "That's not the real him. I don't know him like you know him."

"He treats me like a princess."

"What about the men who follow him?"

"What about them?"

"How do you think they treat their women?"

"Is that my problem?"

"Maybe it should be."

She shook her head as though it would reset the discussion.

"I thought the knife stuff bothered you."

"It does. But that's obviously a little weird. The posts about women sort of go without saying."

"Ha," she scoffed. "I only wish people would stop saying things about it."

"So you're okay with it?"

"He doesn't make me pose for any of them," she shrugged. "I mean, I did once. When we first met. But you couldn't see my face. He was eating sushi off my ass."

"Wilma..."

"With chopsticks," she clarified.

"Do you hear yourself?"

"He treats those other women fine. Just fine. Those are just pictures."

"So he doesn't only pay them," he confirmed. "They stick around."

"We know what we're getting into with Danny. We're not dumb."

"We?"

"I said I was his favorite. I didn't say I was the only one."

Wilma's breathing deepened. She ran a finger beneath her sunglasses to catch a tear before it was exposed, but the residue caught the light.

"You think you're the first to try and make me feel bad about my life?" she asked him.

"Maybe I'll be the last," he tried to keep a light tone.

"Nobody's as smart as they think they are."

She walked away.

"Can I still get a meeting with him?" he called after her.

"He does what he wants," she said over her shoulder. "I'll see what I can do."

"Thank you."

Hart took out his phone and took her word that she wouldn't be in any of the risqué social media photos. He focused on the shots taken of Danny at parties and in public, adding the word "Wilma" to his search. He recognized her from his previous research, but a stronger pattern developed as he found several more images of her and the subject posing in various places around town, looking enough like a couple, but usually with at least a half-dozen other people in tow, clamoring for space in the frame of the picture.

There were men who were running neck-and-neck in the number of times they leered next to Wilma. Hart tried to memorize their faces and look for them at the party so he could engage each in conversation and decide which was the most infatuated with her, and which was easier to manipulate. Ideally, one would fill both roles.

He had a hard time reaching the interview stage, however, as all the young men looked alike to him. He waffled between whether it was due to their faithfulness to a certain style that had taken hold among them, or because he was getting old, and younger people were becoming a nebulous receptacle for his envy, regret, and judgment.

He found himself in Quentin's line of sight at one point in his search, and avoided eye contact after an apologetic grimace.

Quentin was having none of it. He raised his beer bottle before Hart turned away, then approached him while Hart trained his eyes back on him in admonishment.

"Hey," Quentin said as he reached him.

"How large do I have to bulge my eyes?"

"Ah," Quentin waved away his concern. "I'm not worried."

Hart could see that Quentin's beer was merely his latest.

"How many have you had?" he grumbled at him.

"I don't want you to take the fall on your own, Hart. It's not fair."

"You have other people to think about," Hart spoke in quiet, measured tones that he hoped Quentin would imitate.

"Megan can take care of herself."

"What about the…"

Hart stopped short of saying "baby".

Quentin started to laugh. He put his hand up to his ear and leaned in to Hart.

"The what?"

Hart didn't know how to read his laughter.

"Come on," Quentin beckoned him with the hand that held his beer. "You can say it. Megan's not around."

"So she told you?"

Quentin stood up straight and sucked from his bottle.

"She told me what she told you."

"And what's so funny about that?"

"Damn. Is that what my laugh sounded like? Sorry. I was going for remorse. Regret. I wanted to sound rueful. Man, what's up with all those sad R words?"

Hart sunk.

"She didn't, you know…" he couldn't bring himself to say it.

"No," Quentin shook his head. "She didn't do that."

Hart resurfaced.

"Thank God," he took a deep breath.

"There never was a baby."

Quentin waited for a reaction from Hart, but there was nothing to see. He observed a while longer before proceeding.

"She really wanted you to do what you're doing," he said.

"Was it supposed to be me all along?" Hart still betrayed no emotion. "Were you just bait?"

"I wanted to do it," Quentin started to get loud again.

Hart pulled him outside onto an empty section of the deck, not far from where he had spoken to Wilma earlier.

"You were saying?" Hart prompted him after they settled into their positions.

"That first time I approached you," Quentin obliged. "That was real. From the heart. She was glad you turned me down."

"Of course she was."

"Not because she was worried about me," Quentin laughed again, easily capturing the sadness this time. "She thought I would suck at it."

Hart looked out into the canyons ablaze. Fire was now visible along the ridgeline. More planes and helicopters were banking around the smoke.

"You two are a lot alike," Quentin narrated the scene.

Hart looked back at him.

"That was supposed to be a compliment," Quentin explained. "You both have a very strong work ethic. You're both very good at your jobs."

"I told you this isn't a job."

"Semantics."

"This is about Stanley."

With those words, Hart appeared to put himself in a trance. He looked at the canyon as though staring into a campfire. The flames pushed up the smoke, which started to shift in their direction. Ash lightly fell on the deck, and in the pool.

"It is still about Stanley, isn't it?" Hart wanted confirmation.

Quentin tried to give it to him.

"What else would it be about?" he asked, then suspected that was no help whatsoever.

But Hart didn't look upset.

He was too preoccupied with the possibilities.

"Nothing I'd want to admit," he summoned the energy to say.

He waved his hand through the falling ash, then studied the flakes in his palm.

"Do you want to call this off?" Quentin studied him.

Hart paused.

"No."

"So aside from me keeping my distance and meeting you at the car, what's the plan?"

Hart looked at him and lifted a weary grin.

"Sowing the seeds of doubt," he turned his attention back to the fire. "Turning his brownnosers against each other, against him."

"Sounds rather ambitious."

"No more so than what I've pulled off before."

"Are you ever going to tell me those stories?"

Hart glanced back his way.

"We'll see."

They watched the ridgeline together, brushing the ash from in front of their faces, and watched the guests around the pool do the same but loudly, jokingly, with exaggerated movements. The men laughed, the women squealed.

A scream rose above the noise, a sincere expression of horror. It rose again, making it clear it came from inside the house. People stopped what they were doing and tried to trace the source, which wall or window it came through.

Wilma ran into the pool area.

"Someone shot Danny!" she wailed. "He's dead!"

Two women comforted her.

Some men rushed into the house.

"Wow," Quentin said to Hart. "You really are good."

Hart opened his mouth and started to say something, but could only shake his head.

"Shall we still head to the car?" Quentin relished being the one in control.

"Yes," Hart emphatically agreed. "Before we're prevented from leaving."

He had his feet under him again, and led them toward the door.

The bouncers had abandoned their post to follow the screams. Hart and Quentin hurried down the steep cement stairs to the street, taking each step two feet at a time, as though performing a tap dance routine. They came as close to running to the car as they could without running, appearing to silently agree that running would look suspicious. Almost as suspicious as what they were doing.

"We should really just walk," Hart caught on.

"Okay."

"If the cops pass by before we get to the car, we want to look cool, not like we desperately need to find a bathroom."

Quentin laughed harder than the quip warranted.

Hart studied him.

"What?" Quentin noticed.

"You sure are calm."

"I'm in good hands. I trust you."

Hart kept his eyes on him for several more paces. He was about to face forward again when Quentin started to look as nervous as he should have before. Hart checked to see what finally agitated him.

A patrol car with its beacon lights spinning drove slowly up the road toward them.

"They could be old friends of mine," Hart tried calm Quentin.

The car pulled to a stop as it reached them.

"Good afternoon, gentlemen," the driver said as he rolled down the window.

"Officer," Hart nodded.

"You guys evacuating?"

"Oh, you mean from the fire?"

The officers glanced at each other.

"Uh, yeah," the driver said. "From the fire."

"That we are," Hart said. "That we are."

"Well, if you know any of the neighbors, encourage them to get out, too. We just got the word."

"Will do, officer."

Hart offered a casual salute as the car rolled ahead and the officer in the passenger seat started to announce the evacuation over the loudspeaker.

As they continued their walk to the car, Quentin chuckled.

"What?" Hart asked him.

"Real cool," Quentin teased him.

Hart chuckled too, while including a "fuck you."

They made the final turn to where the car was parked.

Two men stood by the line of vehicles along the street. One wore a light cardigan and khakis, while the other was also well-dressed, but of a different fashion, as though on his way to deliver an expensive drug order for the party.

"Are they next to your car?" Hart asked.

"I think so."

The man in the cardigan gave them a friendly wave as they drew closer.

"Hey there," he added.

"Hello," Hart said, less a greeting than a cue to explain their presence.

"Would you please come with me, Bernhart?" the man maintained the same cheery tone.

Hart tensed up, then tried to act as though he was merely surprised.

"My car is only a few doors down," the man continued, as if that was Hart's main concern. "Your son-in-law will drive his own car, and Jep will ride shotgun. And I do mean shotgun, eh Jep?"

The slicker dresser smiled.

Hart turned to Quentin.

"What did you do?"

Quentin recoiled and was about to offer an explanation, but the cardigan man interrupted him.

"Leave that to me, Quentin."

He turned his attention back to Hart.

"Just come with me, B.C., and all will be made clear. But we need privacy. It's evacuation day. The hills have ears."

He smiled broadly.

Hart was still focused on Quentin, resisting the urge to jump him.

"You have nothing to fear," the man said to Hart, trying to talk him down. "I'm a big fan of your work. I want to join forces. Become a real-life Justice League. Or Avengers, if you prefer."

Hart turned to the man in the cardigan. He looked him up and down, pausing at his saddle shoes.

"Nice, eh?" the man noticed. "When was the last time you saw a pair of these? I mean, aside from a bowling alley or golf course. But these are real suede. They remind me of a better time, a less-confusing time, when this country knew what it was."

Hart still didn't move.

Quentin started to sway back and forth.

The voice over the patrol car's loudspeaker grew louder. The car had turned around and was coming back, ordering people to evacuate their homes.

"I guess nobody's called in the hit on Danny boy yet," said the man in the cardigan.

He put his hands on his hips wide enough to reveal a shoulder holster under his sweater, complete with weapon.

"One of the things I love about your style, B.C., is the way you show up to a job unarmed," he narrated the display of his gun.

He crossed his arms, closing the curtains.

"Or someone did call it in," he looked at Jep, "and those officers are just terrible multitaskers."

Jep laughed.

Hart exhaled and went slack.

The man in the saddle shoes read that as his surrender.

"We'll be at the condo," he said to Jep. "Give us some time."

Jep nodded and held the door open for Quentin, who couldn't bring himself to make eye contact with Hart as he lowered himself into the driver's seat.

The man in the cardigan gestured for Hart to join him.

"Just a little farther down the road," he smiled.

The ash was gaining strength, resembling a snowstorm in the sun.

CHAPTER 12

Hart kept quiet in the car, which bore the logo of a rental company.

The man looked over at him intermittently, expecting some questions.

"I'm Rick," he finally said.

"Agent Rick?" Hart replied.

Rick giggled.

"Is it that obvious?"

"You can take off the navy blue suit, but the stick up your ass is permanent."

He giggled harder.

"Agent Rick," he settled down. "I like that. With the first name. Like the pastor of a church. Pastor Rick."

"And Jep?" Hart asked. "I assume he's not Agent Jep."

"Informant Jep. He does a little work on the side for me now and then."

"How far off the books are you on this?"

"I'm out there," Rick winked. "But not as far as you may think."

"I suppose I should be grateful."

"Atta boy."

"What's the catch?"

"Let's wait until we're sitting someplace that isn't moving."

In a matter of minutes, they turned into a recently-completed condominium complex, the units freshly painted, a sales office still on the premises.

Rick announced they had arrived.

"Jep's place?" Hart asked.

"Nope," Rick popped the 'p', and left it at that.

They parked in a space that had "reserved" painted on the pavement, and a unit number painted on the wheel stop. They walked along a cement path that wound between a lawn and a row of oleanders to a door with the corresponding number.

The condo was sparsely furnished with pieces likely purchased from an office supply warehouse. Rick took a seat on one side of a table that stood between the kitchen counter and the living area, where a futon faced a flat-screen television mounted on the wall.

"Funny how these things always seem to wind up at a party thrown by the wealthy and beautiful," he said as he gestured for Hart to sit in the chair across the table from him.

"Why didn't you pick me up before the party?" Hart asked as he sat down. "Why not just come to my house?"

"We thought targeting Danny was a brilliant idea."

"You obviously didn't need me to do it."

"We had to put you there."

"But you didn't trust me to carry it out."

"Should we have?"

"It wasn't my best plan."

"What was it?"

"Quentin didn't tell you?"

"We tried to talk to Quentin as little as possible."

"Well," Hart stumbled into some unexpected laughter, "I was going to turn some of Danny's worshippers against him, more or less."

"Oof," Rick winced. "Glad we intervened."

"Why was taking out Danny a brilliant idea?"

"I take it you studied him pretty carefully in order to come up with that inane plan."

"I did."

"Then you're familiar with how rival gun manufacturers feel about him?"

"They were more embarrassed by him than his own family was."

"Chance Werther in particular."

"Werther will probably throw a parade when he finds out Danny's dead."

"Oh, he'll do something that amounts to dancing on his grave. And we'll make sure everyone knows about it."

Hart recognized the plan.

"These aren't the Hatfields and McCoys. They make guns, they don't fire them at each other like a couple of hillbilly clans in a family feud."

Rick smiled.

"Not unless one of them shoots first. Or appears to."

Hart sighed.

"Which is where I come in."

Rick added a nod to his smile.

"You have a gift," he said.

"You mean the one you're giving me by not hanging me out to dry for Danny's murder?"

"I wouldn't worry about that one. The crime scene is going to burn down by tomorrow morning. Can you believe the timing of that fire?"

Hart agreed with mocking wholeheartedness, a mouth-open smile and disbelieving headshake.

Rick watched him wryly before launching his next move.

"When your grandson died," he said at last, letting the phrase hover before moving on to his point. "I'll bet you hated it when people would say 'It's God's plan.'"

"More than God himself."

"I don't blame you. Awful choice of words. And I say that as a Christian. But I must also say, there may be something to that empty platitude in your case. Oh, the places you've gone. An assassin has to have a bit of the escape artist in them, but you're a regular Harry Houdini."

"Going after Chance Werther will take care of that."

"You've considered him before, I gather."

"For about eleven seconds, until I read about his security forces."

"Force," Rick corrected him. "He only has one."

"With enough firepower to overtake a small country."

"You'll have a team of your own. Over are the days of going it alone."

"You don't need me."

"We want you."

Hart may as well have had a net over him and ropes tied around his wrists and ankles.

"How did you find me?" he asked. "Was it the videos posted by those wackos in front of my daughter's house?"

"Are they still active?"

"I don't know," Hart realized. "I don't visit their site."

"Why would you? Why any functional person?"

Hart enjoyed hearing them mocked.

"I first clocked you from the Great Glenn Caper. We had no jurisdiction. Glenn wasn't exactly a player. Probably a fan of that stupid website. But like a lot of folks, I was fascinated by the case. Unlike a lot of folks, I had access to some really neat-o resources. The proximity of your grandson's school to Glenn's parked car caught my attention. I searched for current or ex-military and law enforcement with ties to the school children. Not to disparage my brothers-in-arms, but we're a good place to start. We can be an angry lot. You and some guy in the Reserves came up. He was out of town for Annual Training during The Glenn Festival. Then the militia massacre happened, and we had full access to that baby, since they were considered a terrorist organization. We went along with the local law enforcement version of events, because really, who gives a shit? But I wondered. And I checked phone records. And you got a signal. Who knew that Podunk town would have such good coverage?"

Hart exhaled and a laugh poked through.

"I didn't bring my phone the first time."

"The time you paid cash at the hotel and signed in as BC Hart?"

Hart nodded.

"Clever pseudonym," Rick chided. "Why are aliases often so similar to the original name?"

"Easier to remember."

"See how valuable you are?" Rick spread his arms toward Hart. "Such keen insights into the criminal mind. So why did you go back?"

"Impulse. A conversation with my daughter."

"So much for insight."

"Patterns are a myth."

"Not true. They led me to you. The personality profile, the phone signal, the lack of a signal during those times when you hit your other targets. All of these things lit up the trail I've been following, more as a fan than an investigator."

"Why the enthusiasm?"

"I think you're onto something. Your idea could save lives in the long run. I thought of it myself years ago, no kidding, but couldn't follow through on it for obvious reasons. Now here you are, making it happen."

"Is there anything in this for me?"

"Other than the satisfaction of continuing the good work you started, but with more help?"

"You think I like doing this?"

"I like that you're doing this," Rick allowed a dash of severity into his tone, then smiled off the harshness.

"If I fail," Hart didn't find the smile comforting. "I'll be left to twist in the wind."

"I'm afraid so," Rick acknowledged. "Though only for whatever case we're pursuing at the time."

"This doesn't end with Werther?"

"We have a list. How far down that list we go? Eh. We'll play it by ear."

"And I get no credit for any of my previous work," Hart wanted verification. "All that stuff you're such a fan of."

"Sorry. The avenging angel narrative doesn't work for us. Makes us look bad. Wouldn't look good for your daughter, either. The public will allow her one rash attack on a gun maker by her grief-stricken father. A string of attacks? She, and her organization, are over."

"So if I live through a job," Hart wanted clarification, "it's whatever story we go in with. For instance, we take out Werther, it's someone from Danny's circle out for revenge. If I die, it's me. It's the crazy grandfather of a school-shooting victim."

"You'll be hailed as a martyr," Rick said, as though trying to convince him to take a bite out of something that tasted better than it looked.

"What am I in the mean time?"

Rick was forced to drop any pretense of promotion.

"A missing person."

Hart let the idea pour over him.

Rick explained further.

"You can write one last letter to each of the most important people in your life. Peaches, Megan, your ex-wife. We'll have Quentin deliver them. He'll say that he woke up one morning, and you were gone. He found the letters on the table in the hotel you were staying at. You'll write about feeling like you want to disappear, that your ex-wife should sell your house, since her name is still on it. You'll implore them not to look for you. That this is for the best. That you haven't been handling Stanley's death in a very healthy manner."

Hart agreed facially with that assessment.

"Aside from those parameters," Rick continued. "Speak from the heart. Tell them how you feel about them. That sort of thing."

Hart looked down at the table. It was brand new, no scratches, no marks. An unscathed coat of shellac shined up at him.

"If I make it through all the jobs you want me to do…" he asked while still staring at the tabletop.

"Sure," Rick anticipated his question. "There's always the chance of a tearful reunion down the road."

Hart looked up from the table and around the room.

"Is this where I'm staying?"

Rick reached his right hand into the right pocket of his cardigan, pulled out a key, and pinned it onto the table with his index finger, sliding it across the surface as far as she could without getting up.

"Fake identity?" Hart asked.

"We've got one ready just in case."

"What's the name?"

"I don't know," Rick shrugged. "It's on a passport in my office somewhere. I think you might be Canadian. Meanwhile, pay cash."

Rick reached into his other pocket and pulled out a small pile of twenty dollar bills, which he placed next to the key.

"There's a shopping center walking distance from here. Maybe five minutes."

"And that's it," Hart said. "That's the deal."

"I thought you'd be more receptive," Rick admitted. "Now that I've finally met you, it seems like blackmail. Still beats any alternatives you have at this point. Even if it didn't, I get the impression you hate yourself enough to take it, anyway.

Hart started to nod rhythmically to a slow beat, almost to a point where Rick may have been compelled to ask him if he was all right. But the silence didn't quite make it that far. Rather than answer, Hart took his wallet out from his back pocket and put it on the table.

"There's a video of Stanley on my phone I like to watch," he said. "When you start cutting my service and wiping away evidence, can you please keep that in there?"

"With pleasure."

Rick took the wallet, emptied the cash and tossed it toward Hart, then stood up to leave.

"I'm looking forward to working with you," he said. "You could say it's a dream come true."

He paused in the doorway before exiting.

"We'll be in touch. On the landline."

Hart seemed willing to do nothing else but wait for the call. He sat in the same chair for hours after Rick left.

The key and the cash sat in the same spot on the table.

When darkness fell, he moved to the futon and turned on the flat screen television. A local news station broadcast footage of the fire. Danny's house had been overtaken by the fire, flames bursting through the windows. His murder was being attributed to looters who were taking advantage of the evacuation. There were no suspects. There was only the idea. Hart listened to the story over and over, and fell asleep.

A knock on the door woke him. He reached over for his phone, which was little more than a clock now, anyway. The battery was dead and he had no charger. The only other clock was on the microwave oven, which was too small and too far away to read. It was nothing but a green light from where he sat.

He looked through the peephole and saw the distorted image of Quentin in the dim light of the lamps that lined the paths of the complex, his forehead three times larger than normal. Hart opened the door and stood on the threshold.

Quentin held up the travel bag Hart had packed in the car.

"Are you allowed to come in?" Hart asked as he took the bag. "Or did Rick tell you to drop it off and leave?"

"Rick?"

"The agent."

"He told me his name was Ron."

Hart chuckled.

"Of course he did. Did he send some paper and a pen over with you?"

"Why?"

"I'm supposed to write letters to the people close to me and lie to them about where I've gone, but be honest with them about how much they mean to me."

"No, I'm afraid..."

Quentin was interrupted by his phone bleating out a text alert. He pulled the phone from his back pocket and read it.

"It's from him."

"God? Or Rick-Ron?"

"Sorry about paper," Quentin read the text aloud. "Walk to store. Will be watching."

Hart walked his bag over to the dinette set and dropped it on the floor before taking some cash and the key from the table.

"Thanks, Rick-Ron!" he announced into the air around him.

Quentin's phone pinged again.

"He says you're welcome."

"He's got a good sense of humor, I'll give him that," Hart said as he walked back toward the door. "Don't say 'thank you', Rick-Ron!"

Quentin's phone responded. He held it up for Hart to see.

Okay I won't, it read.

Hart rolled his eyes.

"I'm suddenly glad I don't have service anymore."

He shut the door behind them and they ventured out.

Quentin said he had seen the shopping center on the way in. It was on a nearby street that was more like a freeway with traffic lights. They were the lone pedestrians as far as they could see, and when they crossed at one of the lights, it took them over twenty seconds to cross the eight lanes that spanned both directions of the boulevard, according to the timer on the walk sign. They didn't speak to each other while they walked, as the din of speeding vehicles made it difficult to hear much else. They waited until they entered the harsh light of the drug store to start up a conversation.

"Is your phone bugged?" Hart asked as they wandered toward the office supply aisle.

"No. Just the condo."

"You sure?"

"I was in possession of my phone the whole time. He never touched it. Unless he has some sort of superpower."

"He doesn't need one. Just your number. But that cardigan does look pretty magical."

They reached the aisle.

"Why do you want to know?" Quentin asked. "Is there something you want to tell me?"

"There's a lot of things I want to tell you. I'm going to tell you. But no, I've got nothing to hide from Rick-Ron. I was just curious."

"Really? I finally get the story?"

Hart reached for a pad of paper.

"I'd rather you hear it from me than Rick-Ron. Besides, I'm not writing you a letter, telling you how much you mean to me, so I figure I owe you something."

"You?" Quentin sounded embarrassed. "Owe me?"

"Don't worry about it," Hart waved away his shame. "You didn't betray me. Agent Cardigan had me in his sights long before he contacted you. I hope he made that clear."

"Not really."

"Not surprising," Hart grabbed a box of pens.

"What is he doing with you?" Quentin asked.

Hart held the box and the pad of paper and stood in the aisle, thinking of an answer.

"He's running with our idea," he decided to say. "Well, it's more my idea now. And he's using me as a human shield. Too bad my idea isn't the kind you can copyright. I could sue him."

"You could do something else."

"Quentin," Hart grinned, "You sly boy. What did you have in mind?"

"Nothing," he looked startled. "I just meant what I said. You could do something else. I don't know what. Sorry."

"I'm kidding," Hart started walking. "This is right where I need to be. I deserve this."

He went to the one cashier on duty to pay. Quentin followed.

When they walked outside, the busy boulevard roared on the other side of the parking lot, which was less than half full, and allowed for some speech.

"I promise I won't read your letters," Quentin said.

"Hadn't crossed my mind, Q. And not because I trust you."

"So...you do trust me?"

"Of course. I'm just not much of a writer. There won't be much to read. I'm going to tell Megan I love her, Peaches I could have loved her, and tell my ex to sell the house."

"And that you loved her at one time."

"We'll see how I'm feeling when the pen hits the paper."

"And you'll tell them all not to look for you."

"That is part of the arrangement."

"They'll ignore you. They'll look."

"They won't for long."

"They care about you."

"That's not what I mean."

The eight lanes' worth of noise started to crest as they drew closer to it. Quentin looked over at Hart for an answer.

"This first job," Hart responded. "I'm not making it out alive."

"Hart..."

"It's not me. There's nothing you should be talking me out of," Hart assured him. "It's them. They'll make sure of it."

"What makes you say that?"

They reached the mound of grass separating the parking lot from the sidewalk. The crosswalk was steps away, and their light was green, but Hart stopped on the modest peak, as though making an announcement.

"Do the math. I live, it looks like a gun manufacturer civil war. Whatever. Where's the rooting interest? The gun haters will scoff. The gun lovers will hate to see Mom and Dad fight. That's been the problem with our idea from day one. Well, one of the problems. It looks like gun owners turning on each other. And like Rick-Ron said about the mountain yahoos, who gives a shit? But now he has a martyr ready to sacrifice. Once I go down, there's the movement."

He proceeded down the grassy slope. The light was red now. He pressed the walk button.

"Why would they wait?" he concluded.

The cars were in motion. The noise swelled. Quentin didn't try to compete with it.

When the light turned, and the crosswalk chirped for the blind and posted the countdown for those who could see, he remained quiet.

He listened to Hart's stories when they arrived back at the condominium. Hart told him about Glenn in great detail, and about the mountain compound. He told him about the gun show parking lot and the social media showoff. He told him about Representative Wayne Raine. He told him about the conversation he had with Megan, and Quentin compared Hart's account to the version Megan told him. He told him about the missions he decided not to pursue, the friendships and the romance he could no longer pursue, and the requirements of being on the agent's leash. Quentin imagined the agent, whatever his name was, listening in.

He fell asleep while Hart wrote his letters.

Hart woke him up and handed him the letters.

They hugged goodbye.

Hart reached inside his bag for the phone charger and plugged it in. He started to watch the video that Stanley took, the six seconds of Hart sitting at his table back home reading the newspaper, and Stanley putting his foot on the table trying to tease his grandpa.

When his phone had enough power, Hart unplugged it and moved to the table. He aimed the phone at the spot where Stanley would have been sitting, and watched that six seconds until the battery ran down and the sun came up.

CHAPTER 13

They told him they would cover him.

They positioned themselves on two different buildings across the street from the restaurant where Werther was conducting business over lunch. Hart was scheduled to take out Werther from close range. He would walk toward the restaurant when the Land Rover pulled up to the valet station, then pass by as the security detail escorted Werther to the vehicle. The rooftop snipers would hit the bodyguards while Hart dropped Werther in the confusion. A car would pull up to retrieve Hart.

"I don't recall any reports of multiple shooters," I said.

"The shooters were there," he said. "They just never fired."

He was lying on the bed closest to the table where I was writing, staring up at the ceiling. He had spent much of our time together in the hotel room pacing, taking laps back and forth between the foot of the other bed and the table. He was wearing down. I could hear it in his voice as well.

"So Hart was right," I said. "They wanted their martyr, and they wanted him right away."

Quentin hummed an affirmative grunt.

I thought of saying, "At least he got Werther," but it sounded crass in my head.

"And he was right about the effect," Quentin said. "What the anti-gun faction was capable of once they had a patron saint."

"Anti-gun faction," I muttered. "Half of them are gun nuts taking advantage of the situation."

"That still gets Rick-Ron and his cronies what they want."

"What have they achieved?"

Quentin took his eyes off the ceiling and looked at me.

"We're sitting in an empty luxury hotel in wine country, aren't we?"

"Gun country."

"The lines have been drawn," he looked back up at the ceiling. "Mission accomplished."

"This was the goal?" I asked.

He nodded.

"Chaos," I confirmed.

"Complete and utter," he said.

"You're just upset."

"I still work for them."

I instinctively looked around the room. Not seeing anything, and not knowing what I was looking for, I looked for an excuse to leave.

"Don't worry," Quentin read the spike in my heart rate. "They don't track me. I help them track others. Potential targets when things get slow and need a boost. I'd like to say they trust me, but I'm pretty sure they leave me alone because they think of me as a wet noodle."

"You certainly took a lot of precautions for someone who isn't tracked."

"Such a nice hotel," Quentin shrugged. "And such a steal at the price."

"But the hoodie and the beard, the jumpiness."

"I kind of let myself go," he said. "Very low job satisfaction. I never realized how important that was to a happy life. Then again, I used to take a lot of things for granted."

"You still work your regular job, too?"

"It's how I have access to so much of what they want," he nodded. "I've become a master at lying to people."

"Megan?"

"Can't remember the last time I told her the truth. She asked me what time it was a while back. I told her. There's that."

"What about me?"

"This is Hart's story, not mine."

"You're in it," I said, and now that his story had caught up with the present, I wanted an estimate on its truth. "Maybe not in it as much as you really were."

"I haven't killed anyone," he stood up.

"You went through a horrible trauma. I wouldn't blame you for anything you may have done afterwards."

"I have nothing to confess," Quentin took a step toward me.

"Then why are you telling me this story?"

Quentin not only stopped moving in my direction, he seemed incapable of movement.

"This is all my fault," he said. "The world we live in. This was my idea. I didn't kill anyone. I killed everyone."

"I think you're giving yourself too much credit."

"I appreciate your condescension..."

"That didn't come out the way..."

"No, really. I do. I get what you mean. I've told myself the same thing in so many words, so many times. Yes, other forces came together to make it happen. But I started it."

He started to sway.

He steadied himself and sat down across the table from me.

I leaned back in my chair.

"What am I supposed to do with this?" I gestured to the notebook in front of me.

"I don't know," Quentin inspected his chair, as if looking for an eject button.

"If what you say is true, or enough of it, I can't publish it without putting my life in danger. I don't know you well enough to do that."

"You could publish it anonymously," he said, giving up his chair inspection and settling in. "You must know someone who could run it on their site. Someone you trust."

"Not without verifying at least some of it. I assume you don't want me to talk to Megan. Obviously Rick-Ron and the crew are out of the question. Who else is there? Peaches? Nando? They were kept in the dark, according to you. Is there anyone who can back you up? Anyone I can talk to?"

Quentin shook his head.

"Then I'm afraid I can't run with it, Quentin. I'm sorry."

He stared at the table. That wasn't low enough, so he stared at the floor.

"I wanted to tell someone," he said at last. "I needed to get this off my chest."

He looked up.

"I'm sorry to burden you," he added.

I didn't doubt him. That he was sorry, or that his story was true. Some artistic liberties were taken, for sure, and memories reconfigured over time. But I believed him.

"The problem," I explained, "is that it's going to sound like some fringe conspiracy theory, one of the thousands lounging around the web. And none of those people are risking their lives to get them out there. They may think they are, if they're delusional..."

Quentin reanimated.

"I could tell you about the next mission," he charged into the idea. "How it will play out. And when it goes according to my prediction, it will vouch for me."

"That doesn't prove anything about the past. Only that you work for Rick-Ron."

"You're right," he said, but with conviction rather than disappointment.

He leaned forward, looking more like the tech administrator than the paranoid fugitive on self-imposed exile.

"Give me a few days," he said, almost absent-mindedly in deference to the thoughts tumbling toward a whole. "I'll have proof. A test that keeps everyone safe."

He meant everyone but himself. I should have known that. I probably did know that. But I wanted the story.

They were probably not very enthusiastic about his plan at first. He was valuable to them. But they could probably see he was becoming less valuable. He was past done, only managing to do the work they assigned him out of habit and remorse. His tasks were lamentations.

He set up a meeting with Rick-Ron, whose name he still didn't know, and whose identity Quentin could never uncover, for all his technical expertise and access. He surmised Rick-Ron probably wasn't even an agent, but under contract by someone who was, or used to be.

"We appreciate your role in setting up the next big thing," Rick-Ron said to Quentin, more or less. "But aside from your importance to us, and the risk of involving you as deeply as you're suggesting, you know the parameters on this one."

"I know. Muslims only."

"Arabic Muslims. They have to look the part."

"I helped you build the roster," Quentin reminded him. "And I can add even more value by putting myself on it."

"Nothing adds more value. A mentally-disturbed white man only gets us so far. No offense."

"For what, the mentally disturbed part?"

"I'm merely parroting what the press would run with."

"None taken."

"We've played the long game," Rick-Ron further clarified. "Now we're pressing the proverbial detonator. Angry white people with guns get people thinking. Angry Muslims with guns get people shitting their pants."

"So let's celebrate diversity," Quentin was determined. "Picture this: Ted Foucault, the president of the largest gun lobby, gets taken out not only by a band of Muslims, but a radicalized American. A radicalized American father of the same child whose grandfather is patron saint of the anti-gun lobby. Now that's a kick-ass sleeper cell.

We'll have this country vibrating like a tuning fork. I've got the beard, I've got the anger, I've got the hatred of your employer."

"Jealousy among the saints," Rick-Ron teased him.

"I don't want sainthood. I want out."

Rick-Ron approved.

Quentin called me with the news. I almost didn't answer since the Caller ID read "Leroy Ranch BBQ", then realized Quentin was likely using the restaurant's phone to stay off of his own. He was also, as it turned out, treating himself to a celebratory brisket sandwich.

He rushed through the generalities of his conversation with Rick-Ron and the plan they agreed on, not because of paranoia in wanting to keep the call short, but thanks to his excitement. During an especially large bite of his sandwich that forced him to slow down, he decided it would be best to allow some time for the future to sink in, so that he may discuss what was to come in more measured tones.

He asked me to meet him at the hotel.

"Our hotel," he called it.

He gave me a date and time.

When I showed up, he wasn't there.

A man wearing a cardigan, khakis, and saddle shoes sat at our table instead.

"Rick?" I asked. "Ron?"

"Let's go with Ray," he grinned. "The Three Rs."

"Quentin said he wasn't being monitored."

"Q was slipping. I'm sure you noticed, thanks to your razor sharp reporter's instincts."

He offered me the seat across from him, where Quentin had sat last time.

"So he's in," I confirmed.

"He's in."

"You're sacrificing him. Like you sacrificed Hart."

"You're the one he wants to impress. I hope you believe his story now that he's willing to die for it."

"Not that I can publish it."

"Go ahead," he shrugged. "It hardly matters. The world has moved on from truth. There are only beliefs. For everyone who buys what Quentin had to say, there will be another who does not, who has a favorite story of their own they hold dear."

"I understand the concept of creating a world so wild with guns it causes people to consider disarming," I said. "But you seem to be making that harder the wilder you make it."

"I'm sorry," he waved his hands and smiled as he shook his head, as though trying unsuccessfully to order dinner in a foreign language. "I guess Q didn't make it clear before. Getting rid of guns is no longer the goal."

"It's not?"

"Frankly it never was. I mean, it was for Quentin. It was for Hart. Maybe for me, for a while. Definitely not for the rest of my colleagues. They set me straight."

"What is it, then?" I guided him back on track.

"The people can have all the guns they want. Stockpiles if they're so inclined. So long as The Man can keep an eye on them."

"The Man," I scoffed.

"Corny, I know. But I'm old-fashioned. And I want to keep our names out of this."

"So a gun registry..." I prompted him.

"A full-blown surveillance state," he corrected me. "An upgrade in our capabilities with a downgrade on our constraints. A blow-by-blow biography on every boring one of us. And we will surrender authorship of our stories to make sure our neighbors stay as boring as we are. Our debates over privacy will seem so quaint when we look back on them. 'Grandpa, did everyone have something to hide when you were a kid?'"

"That argument is not going away."

"Maybe in your mind, and the others in your hive. But the rest of us, we're nearly there. We've climbed a pile of guns from nut, to nut provider, to president of the nuts. All those who claim to bear arms in the name of liberty will have compromised that freedom with their passion."

I had a hard time reconciling the enormity of the plan with how simple it was.

I settled into a smaller part of it, something I could grasp.

"Quentin said he was going to tell me the details of his mission."

"He's busy training," he said. "I'd be happy to fill you in. You need an ending, after all."

"Does he know it's his ending?"

"He does."

"And he's okay with it?"

"He's elected himself leader of the gang. Created an online trail that reveals him to be the American turncoat responsible."

"He didn't say anything to me about giving his life."

"I'll bet he did. In so many words."

If he actually did bet me, I wouldn't take him up on it. I would lose. He probably had audio proof.

"What exactly is going to happen?" I asked.

"Magnificence. A full-blast assault on Foucault's home by a sleeper cell of Muslims, both homegrown and here illegally, led by a radicalized tech executive."

He couldn't help but laugh.

"Sorry," he managed through his cackles. "That's the first time I've explained it out loud to someone. Wow. Imagine the frenzy afterwards. That may be even more spectacular. As if we could top a firefight on the front lawn of the most powerful gun lobbyist in America. Can't wait to see the movie. And the series. And the graphic novel. And the books. Oh, the books. I won't be able to keep up. I'm afraid your story will be buried in an avalanche of other hot takes. Which reminds me, there is one stipulation we have when it comes to your entry."

He waited for me to give him his cue.

I was too overwhelmed to give him anything more than some raised eyebrows.

He ran with them.

"You have to wait until the action is over before you publish, assuming you still want to. Predicting the attack on Foucault ahead of time would eventually draw a lot of attention to your work once people started to notice the timeline. If there's one thing we can all still agree on, it's time."

"How are you going to stop me?"

The Three Rs smiled.

"Just don't do it."

He bongo-drummed the table for a couple of beats and stood up, putting a hand on my shoulder as he passed by on his way out. The door shutting added a final bass note.

I suspected the cardigan, khakis, and saddle shoes were a costume, worn only when he met with any of us in person. I wondered if he had considered smoking a pipe as well.

I pulled out my phone. The sound of Quentin's voice would be all the proof I needed.

I tapped to check my audio recordings. They had been wiped clean.

CHAPTER 14

The news had not broken.

Quentin had disappeared, waiting offstage to become a figure as infamous as his father-in-law.

Any adjective would work to describe what was to happen. No portrayal could top the event itself. Sometimes I felt as much like laughing about it as the Three Rs did. Knowing the people involved kept me from reaching that laughter, though. Even more than knowing what the world would look like in the aftermath.

Not that I really knew them. I had only met Quentin, and he spent most of our time together talking about the others. All those people on their way to not being people anymore. They would be characters drawn by everyone who heard about them. Everyone would re-write them each time they thought of them or talked about them. Everyone would feel like they knew them because they had thought a lot about them. It would be a pastime. Building a version of them would be something to do, something that could help explain our own lives in a way that suited our demands.

I couldn't do that to them. Knowing their stories so well, coming as close to the truth as anyone could, made me feel as though I didn't have the right to make sense of them. I thought of how the expert is an expert because he knows there is always more to learn, and is never satisfied with his knowledge.

I wanted to contact Megan. I wasn't sure what I would say to her. Maybe I simply wanted to see that she existed.

She had resigned her position as an advocate. Quentin hadn't told me, but it had been in the news following Hart's suicide assassination of Werther. I hadn't remembered her doing so. It would have been an easy item to overlook in the furor surrounding Hart's martyrdom, but a web search convinced me I must have known. There were no sentences devoted to her moving, so I assumed she was still in town.

I didn't know where she and Quentin lived, but I knew which street led out of the city limits in their direction, based on the story I had been told.

I parked along that street in the mornings and evenings, times when people were inclined to run errands, and I looked at the drivers to see if anyone resembled her. Quentin never described her, but there were plenty of photos online. I brought my notes from Quentin with me, and studied them between vehicles passing by.

It was harvest season, so most were large trucks pulling bins filled with grapes by the ton, which made my search easier, as I could cross off the big rigs from my line of sight at a glance. The street was marked with red streaks left by clusters of grapes falling from the bins.

I considered a way to outline the story, cross-referencing my notes with a fresh pad of paper. I used the clean sheets to construct a frame, a structure for all of Quentin's pacing.

On the second morning, I saw her through a windshield. I needed some time to put aside my work and turn my car around to follow her, but had no trouble picking up her vehicle in the small-town traffic. Her tinted back window still bore a decal with the name and logo of the advocacy group she had worked for.

She drove downtown and parked in front of the coffee house, the same one Hart had haunted with Nando and Peaches.

I was going to catch her before she went inside. I parked across the street and waited as she opened the door to the backseat and leaned inside. I didn't want to startle her when she popped back up.

She emerged holding a car seat with a baby tucked into it.

I stayed put.

She hoisted the seat by the handle, swung it alongside her hip, and carried it all inside.

I processed what I had seen before following her.

She sat by herself at a table for four, allowing plenty of room to place the car seat on the table. She talked to the baby wide-eyed and in a loud whisper, the way people do, telling the baby how sweet and beautiful it is.

I imagined for a moment yet another twist in the tale Quentin told me about Megan's pregnancy. Then I did the math, based on a baby less than a year old, and realized this life staring back at Megan had nothing to do with the other one featured in the story, whether that other life had been made up or not.

The baby's stare cracked into a grin.

Megan's delight nearly reached a squeal. She looked my way with an apology.

"It's not like he's never smiled at me," she said. "That's probably the tenth time this morning."

I could only grin and offer a reassuring hand flap. I realized I had no coffee on my table.

I wouldn't need any if I decided to talk to her.

She turned her attention back to the baby.

I walked to the counter to order something.

I left my notebook and some paper napkins on the table as a placeholder, which wasn't necessary. There were plenty of tables. But I liked the view from where I was sitting. I felt as though I had spotted an actor from a film that had a profound effect on me, and I wasn't sure how to tell her without sounding like a typical fan, or a stalker.

As I settled back into my seat, I heard her say "Hello" and thought perhaps she was offering me a chance.

I looked up and saw an older woman enter, about the age Megan's mother might be.

"Hi, sweetie," the woman said as they hugged before turning their adoration toward the baby.

"Say hello to Auntie Peaches," Megan cooed to her child.

I was star struck. It wasn't only an actor now, it was a band, and I had a backstage pass. I buried the prospect of talking to them in my coffee and my notes, pretending to be absorbed in both, while listening to their conversation and glancing furtively at their table whenever I felt I could do so with sufficient calm and a length of time that was short but not shifty.

They spoke of Megan's son, foods and toys he liked, noises and movements he made. Megan imitated the noises. Peaches listened as though the stakes could not be higher, like she was sure an answer was about to be revealed, the answer to every question she ever had. The baby was the quiet type, surveying the world with an intensity that matched Peaches'.

They didn't speak of Hart, or Quentin. Not that morning. They were far more interested in each other. The small, inflatable dramas featuring things they had bought, errands they had run, people they had bumped into, and the hassles involved in all of the above. I tried to take notes on their talk, but the details were so trite, they weren't worth writing down.

I was jealous nonetheless. Their conversation was shallow but it was beautiful. The baby would contribute a gentle grunt and they would stop mid-sentence, praising and exalting the sound.

They called him "Laz."

I suspected it was short for Lazarus, which struck me as a bit much, but it did make for that cute abbreviated version.

"You realize he'll probably go with 'Russ' when he gets older," Peaches confirmed my suspicion about the full name at one point.

I also agreed with her. He would run with the second part of his name, just like his grandfather Bernhart had.

I wanted to join their conversation. Not to confirm any of Quentin's stories, or to warn them their lives were about to be fed to the public again. I wanted to join them because it would feel good.

But I didn't know how.

I wasn't sure I could talk without trying to say something, without trying to make a larger claim about the bigger picture we live in. I wondered when I last spoke about anything that wasn't in some way an argument.

I stopped worrying about my role and listened. My concern gave way to enjoyment at what I was hearing and, occasionally, seeing. I only wished that Hart and Quentin were there with them.

Of course, if they were there, that would mean they had thought better of their plan, and risen above it. Their victims would still be alive. The meeting in the hotel would not have been necessary. I wouldn't know them. I wouldn't know their story. Their loss and their pain wouldn't be written in my handwriting on the papers in front of me. It would just be them in front of me.

Megan and Quentin would simply be a couple out with their baby boy. I would assume both Peaches and Hart were the grandparents, meeting the kids for coffee. Maybe I would pick up on the nature of the older couple's relationship if I noticed Megan calling Hart "Dad" and Peaches by her name. I would notice because their warmth would catch my attention, their enjoyment of each other's company. I would be more inclined to strike up a conversation with them. Only then might I learn about Stanley. If that happened, if they were willing to share their story, I would tell them I had reported on the incident, and was well-versed in its horrors. I would tell them how much I admire their strength, how comforting it is to see the healing power of love revealed in their lives.

"Excuse me," Megan said.

She was looking at me.

So was Peaches.

And I was looking at them.

"Are you okay?" she asked.

I blinked and was surprised by some tears that had collected in my eyes. I shuddered as if I had spilled my coffee.

"I'm sorry," I grabbed a paper napkin and wiped them.

"It's all right," Peaches chimed in. "What's the old expression? A penny for your thoughts?"

"Well," I started to round up my notebook and pen, "that's about what they're worth."

"Don't leave on our account," Megan said.

"I was about ready, anyway," I assured them.

"Are you sure?" Peaches asked. "You're welcome to join us."

I stood and hesitated. This was my chance.

I wondered if it was worth taking.

"No," I said. "But thank you. For everything."

They looked at each other.

"For everything?" Megan spoke to their confusion, and only then did I realize my slip.

"Yes," I stalled by grabbing my napkins and cup from the table and dropping them in the wastebasket near the door. I stood humbly before them as I finalized what to say.

"Thank you for reminding me how beautiful an ordinary day is."

I bowed my head and exited before I could see their reactions.

I sat in the car and wondered if I had made the right move, if I should go back inside and tell them all that I knew.

I decided it was too late. In every regard, it was too late.

Telling them what was to come wasn't going to stop it from happening, which was a good reason to keep quiet. Knowing the future would leave them feeling helpless, adding an unnecessary layer to their grief when Quentin's life was added to the lore.

I even toyed with the idea that they already knew everything. They were in on it somehow, and withholding the information had saved me from Rick, or Ron, or Ray, or someone else I had yet to meet. There was no true villain, after all. No head. No public enemy. There was the public itself. Millions of pieces taking individual cues from a violent whole.

Megan and Peaches walked out together.

I slouched behind the steering wheel in case they looked my way.

Peaches held the baby against her chest while Megan fit the car seat back into its base, kissing his little head while she listened to Megan talk.

I had done the right thing.

Megan finished setting up the seat. Peaches nuzzled the round, fuzzy head before handing him to Megan.

I had nothing to offer them.

Megan finished strapping Laz into his seat. She and Peaches hugged each other.

They knew what to do, no matter what happened.

They separated, then hugged each other again.

Maybe Peaches helped Megan understand. Maybe Megan had known all along, and needed Peaches to remind her.

I couldn't hear them all that well with my windows rolled up, but as their conversation reached its conclusion, I distinctly heard each of them say the same thing to one another.

"I love you."

Also by Sean Boling

The Current Mr. Orr
Devin's Best Afterlife
Once in Two Lifetimes
Revenge and Wellness in the Sweet Hereafter

Standalone
Cut Flowers
Abraham the Anchor Baby Terrorist
Pigs and Other Living Things
The Summer of Our Foreclosure
Satellite Campus
A Charter to That Other Place
The Latest Version of My Love Story
Show Them What They Won
The Name Field
Should
Moral Adjacent
Over Here We Have

About the Author

Sean lives with his family in Templeton, California. He teaches English at Cuesta College.